Acting Edition

I0600527

Gutenberg!
The Musical!

by Anthony King &
Scott Brown

concord
theatricals

FOR PRODUCTION INQUIRIES

UNITED STATES AND CANADA
info@concordtheatricals.com
1-866-979-0447

UNITED KINGDOM AND EUROPE
licensing@concordtheatricals.co.uk
020-7054-7298

Each title is subject to availability from Concord Theatricals Corp., depending upon country of performance. Please be aware that *GUTENBERG! THE MUSICAL!* may not be licensed by Concord Theatricals Corp. in your territory. Professional and amateur producers should contact the nearest Concord Theatricals Corp. office or licensing partner to verify availability.

This work is published by Concord Theatricals Corp.

No one shall make any changes in this title(s) for the purpose of production. No part of this book may be reproduced, stored in a retrieval system, scanned, uploaded, or transmitted in any form, by any means, now known or yet to be invented, including mechanical, electronic, digital, photocopying, recording, videotaping, or otherwise, without the prior written permission of the publisher. No one shall share this title(s), or any part of this title(s), through any social media or file hosting websites.

For all inquiries regarding motion picture, television, online/digital and other media rights, please contact Concord Theatricals Corp.

THIRD-PARTY MATERIALS USE NOTE

Licensees are solely responsible for obtaining formal written permission from copyright owners to use copyrighted third-party materials (e.g., incidental music not provided in connection with a performance license, artworks, logos) in the performance of this play and are strongly cautioned to do so. If no such permission is obtained by the licensee, then the licensee must use only original materials and materials that the licensee owns and controls. Licensees are solely responsible and liable for clearances of all third-party copyrighted materials, and shall indemnify the copyright owners of the play(s) and their licensing agent, Concord Theatricals Corp., against any costs, expenses, losses and liabilities arising from the use of such copyrighted third-party materials by licensees. For music, please contact the appropriate music licensing authority in your territory for the rights to any incidental music not provided in connection with a performance license.

IMPORTANT BILLING AND CREDIT REQUIREMENTS

If you have obtained performance rights to this title, please refer to your licensing agreement for important billing and credit requirements.

GUTENBERG! THE MUSICAL! is a musical written by Scott Brown and Anthony King. Brown and King developed the show at the Upright Citizens Brigade Theatre in New York City, where it ran for over a year with direction by Charlie Todd and musical direction by Barry Wyner. The cast was as follows:

DOUG SIMON . . . . Anthony King
BUD DAVENPORT . . . . Scott Brown
CHARLES . . . . Barry Wyner
BROADWAY PRODUCER . . . . Ken Keech, Doug Rand

GUTENBERG! THE MUSICAL! was part of the 2005 and 2006 New York Musical Theatre Festival and ran at the Jermyn Street Theatre in London in January 2006. The show opened Off-Broadway on December 3, 2006, at 59E59 and then transferred to The Actors' Playhouse on January 16, 2007. The production closed on May 6, 2007. The Off-Broadway production was directed by Alex Timbers with music direction by T.O. Sterrett. The cast was as follows:

DOUG SIMON . . . . Jeremy Shamos
BUD DAVENPORT . . . . Christopher Fitzgerald
CHARLES . . . . T.O. Sterrett
BROADWAY PRODUCER . . . . Ryan Karels

GUTENBERG! THE MUSICAL! was produced on Broadway by Ambassador Theatre Group, Patrick Catullo, Bad Robot Live, Seth A. Goldstein, Isaac Robert Hurwitz, Runyonland Productions, Kristin Caskey, Mike Isaacson, and Bee Carrozzini, opening at the James Earl Jones Theatre on October 12, 2023. The production was directed by Alex Timbers, with music supervision by T.O. Sterrett, scenic design by Scott Pask, costume design by Emily Rebholz, lighting design by Jeff Croiter, and sound design by Cody Spencer and M.L. Dogg. The production stage manager was Rachel Sterner. The cast was as follows:

DOUG SIMON . . . . Andrew Rannells
BUD DAVENPORT . . . . Josh Gad
CHARLES . . . . Marco Paguia
BROADWAY PRODUCER . . . . Various, including:
    Audra McDonald, Steve Martin, Martin Short, Hillary Clinton, Nathan Lane, and many, many more

CHARACTERS

DOUG SIMON
BUD DAVENPORT
CHARLES

A NOTE ON THE SHOW

This is not the story of Johann Gutenberg. It is the story of Bud & Doug.

DOUG SIMON is an innocent. Naïve, utterly sincere, and earnest, Doug never met a cause he wasn't passionate about. He's a jack of all trades, master of none, who compensates with an infectious, matter-of-fact energy and focus that would sound condescending if he weren't so guileless and likable. He's incredibly proud of the show he wrote with Bud, and thinks Bud, whom he adores, is a genius.

BUD DAVENPORT is an innocent. He's eager to please, and thrives on approval. When Bud sings one of his songs, he's reveling in his own "brilliance." But he's too naïve to be entitled or a true egomaniac; if anything, he's too grateful for the mere opportunity to create and perform. Bud enjoys getting caught up in Doug's passion and admires his friend's Big Ideas.

CHARLES is the pianist and the leader of the band (if you have a band).

Tonight is the most important night of their lives.

A NOTE ON THE SHOW WITHIN THE SHOW

Bud & Doug play a number of roles in the show. But Bud & Doug are not *actors*. This does not mean they should fail. The laughs in the show aren't derived from their falling-short or humiliating themselves; the laughs come from their utter *commitment* to every moment they have written and polished and (probably over-) rehearsed. They believe the show is *working*; they believe every moment is landing as designed. *Trust them.*

Bud & Doug are, at all times, *authors first* – fully aware of the audience and eager to communicate their precious lines, lyrics, and choices. They desperately want the audience to understand the "intelligence" and passion behind it all. They don't trust the audience to infer or deduce anything; they deliver every detail and lesson and moral directly, with (they believe) no ambiguity. When deciding how to play specific actions and moments in the show within the show, it's always best to ask "What would Bud & Doug do?" and "How would Bud & Doug do it?" Keep the answers to these questions close to the surface.

While Bud & Doug do create specific characters for all the parts they play – complete with strong vocal and physical choices – they should never fully disappear into the roles. They're not seasoned performers; they're not trained clowns. They're artists. With a *Message*.

Most important, remember this: To Bud & Doug, the show-within-the-show is not a comedy. It is *important*. It is tragic. It is epic and grand. It should be played with absolute sincerity.

MUSICAL NUMBERS

ACT ONE

1. Prologue
2. Schlimmer
3. I Can't Read
4. Haunted German Wood
5. The Press
6. I Can't Read (Reprise)
7. Biscuits
8. What's The Word
9. Stop The Press
10. Tomorrow Is Tonight

ACT TWO

11. Second Prologue
12. Words, Words, Words
13. Monk With Me
14. Go To Hell
15. Festival
16. We Eat Dreams

ACT ONE

*(**CHARLES** enters, stands center stage and reads from a card.)*

CHARLES. Good evening and welcome to the [BLANK] Theatre. *(**CHARLES** should say the actual name of the theatre.)* For your convenience, bathrooms are available. Now please put your cellphones on vibrate and welcome to the stage, Doug Simon and Bud Davenport.

*(**BUD DAVENPORT** and **DOUG SIMON** enter, nervous but covering with big energy.)*

DOUG. Okay! Here we go.

BUD. So many people!

DOUG. Welcome to GUTENBERG!

BUD. GUTENBERG...THE MUSICAL!

DOUG. My name is Mr. Doug Simon.

BUD. And I am Mr. Bud Davenport.

DOUG. And we have written...a musical.

BUD. *(Rapidly, under his breath.)* Oh my god, I'm so excited.

DOUG. And tonight we are going to present our musical to all of you...for the first time.

BUD. But hopefully not the last time!

DOUG. No! With any luck, we are hoping to take our show to Broadway!

BUD. Our nation's capital!

DOUG. Yes!

BUD. Now as many of you may already know, there are with us in the audience tonight some very big Broadway producers.

DOUG. Chances are, if you don't know the person sitting beside you – they're probably a Broadway producer.

BUD. So tell them to produce our show!

DOUG. Yes.

BUD. Please.

DOUG. Renting this theatre was…incredibly expensive.

BUD. Luckily I have an uncle who recently started hang-gliding. And then recently stopped hang-gliding.

DOUG. It was very quick and he didn't suffer. Which is exactly how I hope all of you die.

BUD. Thanks, Doug. He left me some money and we used all of it to be on this stage. For one night.

DOUG. Plus parking.

BUD. We could not find street parking.

DOUG. So as you can see, we need this to go well.

BUD. It has to.

DOUG. Now, before we get started, we do want to be professional, so – a few introductions.

BUD. Over there with the fancy instruments – the tri-county's premiere wedding band, The Magnificent Seven!*

DOUG. *(After applause –)* We could only afford three of them.

BUD. Yes. But they are "professional musicians." Hit it!

---

* See alternate dialogue on page 90 for productions using only a pianist.

(The band JAMS HARD – on a classic rock song. It's awesome.* **BUD** *dances. Then* **DOUG** *cuts them off with a conductor's flourish –)*

DOUG. STOP! STOP! STOP!

(Then, to audience.) If they play even one more note we have to pay for the song.

BUD. And we have literally no more money.

(A slight blip of panic between them. Then –)

DOUG. Now...writing a musical...is not easy.

BUD. Hats off to you, Elton John.

DOUG. But we did it! I wrote what we call the book of the musical.

BUD. The script.

DOUG. Yes.

BUD. And I wrote the music.

DOUG. The score.

BUD. And the songs.

DOUG. Beautiful songs!

BUD. Thank you. And the lyrics, well...

DOUG & BUD. We wrote those together!

DOUG. Now you're probably sitting there and thinking to yourself, "Okay, so you wrote a show, but what is it about?"

---

* Music for this moment is not included in the score materials for *GUTENBERG! THE MUSICAL!* A license to produce *GUTENBERG! THE MUSICAL!* does not include a performance license for any third-party or copyrighted music. Licensees should create an original composition or use music in the public domain. For further information, please see the Music and Third-Party Materials Use Note on page iii.

BUD. *(For the audience's benefit – infomercial.)* I don't know, Doug – you wrote the script, why don't you tell us?

DOUG. Alright, I will. It's about Johann Gutenberg!

BUD. *(For the audience's benefit – infomercial.)* Who's he?

DOUG. Well, he's the guy who invented the printing press.

BUD. And then printed up a bunch of copies of the Bible.

DOUG. Yes! But what else did he do?

BUD. We did some research to find out.

DOUG. Google! We typed in Johann Gutenberg and printed out the first thing that came up. Read it, Bud!

BUD. *(Reading from paper from his pocket.)* "Gutenberg comma Johann. German printer born around the year 1400. Detailed records of his life and work are scant."

DOUG. Scant? Clearly research was not going to help us.

BUD. Right. So we took a different approach. Historical Fiction.

DOUG. *(For the audience's benefit – infomercial.)* Yes, but what is Historical Fiction?

BUD. *(The definition:)* It's fiction...that's true.

DOUG. Now, normally when you go see a hit Broadway musical you usually expect to see a lot of amazing things. Things like...animal puppets!

BUD. Turntables!

DOUG. Flying cars! And flying car*pets*!

BUD. And so many people pretending to be pop stars.

DOUG. Well, there's a bunch of those things in this show too. But tonight you're gonna have to use your imagination to see them. For example, "Hey Bud – where you going?"

BUD. *(Walks in place.)* Nowhere Doug. I'm on a turntable.

DOUG. Imagination! Now what you're going to see tonight is what we call a reading of a musical.

BUD. *(For the audience's benefit – infomercial.)* Yes, but what is a reading of a musical?

DOUG. *(Joke.)* Does it mean we're going to give you copies of the script so you can read it?

BUD. No.

DOUG. Of course not! No, what it means is there's no set, no costumes, just a few props – and every light they would let us rent from Dance Party DJs dot com. Also? There's no cast.

BUD. It's just me and Doug.

DOUG. Right! We're gonna perform all the roles, sing all the songs, and give you some help to understand the potential of what we've written.

BUD. I think the key word here is "potential."

DOUG. I also like the word "help."

BUD. Now there are an awful lot of characters in this show.

DOUG. How will we differentiate?

BUD. Great question!

> *(They move upstage to a table covered in a sheet, and dramatically remove the sheet to reveal it's full of hats.)*

Using these hats! Aren't they beautiful?!

DOUG. Bud spent three days at FedEx Kinko's.

BUD. They thought I was insane.

> *(**BUD** hands the **BOOTBLACK** hat to **DOUG**. He holds the **WOMAN** hat.)*

DOUG. Is this insane? When I wear this hat –

(*He puts it on, "in character.")* – I'm a Bootblack.

BUD. And I'm –

(*He puts it on, "in character.")* – a Woman.

DOUG. *(Takes his hat off.)* But only for tonight. In an actual production, we would never cast a man to play a woman.

BUD. *(Takes his hat off.)* Representation matters.

DOUG. Now, you're going to see that this show is set in olden times – that means many of the characters will talk like this:

BUD. *(English accent.)* Cheerio!

DOUG. *(English accent.)* Can I help you carry your bucket?

(*They bow.)*

BUD. Also many of the characters in this show cannot read.

DOUG. Of course, that all changes with the climactic invention of

DOUG & BUD. The printing press!

DOUG. Now just before we get started, we do want to take a second to talk about something pretty serious. Every important musical has to tackle at least one incredibly serious issue.

BUD. Like racism.

DOUG. Homophobia.

BUD. Or a man with half a face.

DOUG. Our show is set in Germany. So our serious issue... is Nazis.

BUD. History – and every Indiana Jones movie except *Crystal Skull* – has taught us that Nazis...are not cool.

DOUG. No. They are hateful and they are ignorant. And that ignorance...is in this show.

BUD. It has to be.

DOUG. Because it makes our show important.

> *(Beat.)*

DOUG & BUD. GUTENBERG, THE MUSICAL!

> *(NOTE: Throughout the show* **BUD** *and* **DOUG** *will speak their show's stage directions.)*

BUD. *(Stage direction.)* Prologue: *(He then gestures to* **CHARLES.***)*

[MUSIC NO. 1 – PROLOGUE]

The lights rise on the squalid, stinky bedroom of a Friend of Gutenberg.

DOUG. *(Stage direction.)* The roof is made of dirty thatch. In the corner there are rats gnawing on stinky cheese, and lying absolutely still in the middle of the room without moving is a Dead Baby!

BUD. *(Stage direction.)* Gutenberg's Friend and the Doctor examine the Dead Baby.

DOCTOR (DOUG). Well, we did all we could. I'm afraid your baby is dead.

FRIEND OF GUTENBERG (BUD). Dead? But I gave him this medicine.

> *(***FRIEND** *holds up a jar of jellybeans clearly labeled with the word "JELLYBEANS.")*

DOCTOR (DOUG). Them ain't medicine. Them's jellybeans.

FRIEND OF GUTENBERG (BUD). Jellybeans? But...

DOCTOR (DOUG). If only you could read. See ya!

    *(**DOCTOR** exits.)*

FRIEND OF GUTENBERG (BUD). *(A bit too dramatically.)*
    JELLYBEANS
    NOT MEDICINE
    IF ONLY I COULD READ
    MY SON, HE WOULDN'T NEED...
    AN ELEGY

    STUPID BEANS!
    NOT MEDICINE!
    OH GOD, HERE IN THIS JAR
    I CAN'T READ WHAT THESE ARE
    DAMN JELLY BEANS!

GUTENBERG (DOUG). *(Grand, swaggering entrance.)* Hello Friend, is there anything Johann Gutenberg can do?

FRIEND OF GUTENBERG (BUD). Can you bring a dead baby back to life?

GUTENBERG (DOUG). I don't...think so...?

DOUG. *(Stage direction.)* Friend of Gutenberg sobs like a woman. He cradles his Dead Baby in his illiterate arms. BLACKOUT! Act One, Scene One:

[MUSIC NO. 2 – SCHLIMMER]

Schlimmer, Germany! A German town! Full of German things – like sausages and short pants. Gutenberg walks down the dirt streets of this medieval burg and encounters a Woman and her Daughter on their way to market. They're carrying kraut. Sauerkraut.

WOMAN (BUD). Good morning, Mister Gutenberg!

GUTENBERG (DOUG). Call me Johann! Johann Gutenberg.

DAUGHTER (BUD). Hello, Mister Butengerg.

GUTENBERG (DOUG). It's Gutenberg! How are you today, little girl?

DAUGHTER (BUD). As happy as I *can* be...considering *I can't read.*

DOUG. *(Stage direction.)* Another Woman throws open her shutters to greet the morning. She dumps her stinky chamber pot and suddenly the town of Schlimmer is alive – not alive like a monster, but alive like a town!

(They throw confetti.)

ANOTHER WOMAN (BUD).
IT'S NICE TO LIVE IN MEDIEVAL GERMANY
IN THE BEAUTIFUL TOWN OF SCHLIMMER
WE ALL GET ALONG IN PERFECT HARMONY

BEEF FAT TRIMMER (DOUG).
I'M A BEEF FAT TRIMMER.
THE BEEF COMES IN ALL WHITE WITH FAT
IT LEAVES A GOOD BIT SLIMMER

TWO DRUNKS (BUD & DOUG).
WE'RE JUST DRUNKS COMING HOME FROM THE BAR
IN THE BEAUTIFUL TOWN OF SCHLIMMER!

DRUNK #2 (DOUG). Hey Gutenberg! Got any wine?

DRUNK #1 (BUD). You're the wine presser – tell us where the wine is.

DRUNK #2 (DOUG). Is it over here?

DRUNK #1 (BUD). It's NOT over here!

GUTENBERG (DOUG). Hey now fellas, my wine isn't the answer to all of your problems.

DRUNK #1 (BUD). Yes it is!

DRUNK #2 (DOUG). Drinking your wine is the only thing that makes our terrible lives worth living!

(**TWO DRUNKS** *do a happy dance while they sing.*)

TWO DRUNKS (BUD & DOUG).
GUTENBERG!
DARN TOOTIN'-BERG
HE'S THE BEST CHAP AROUND
AT LEAST IN THIS TOWN
SURE AS SHOOTIN'-BERG!

GUTENBERG (DOUG). Call me Johann.

DRUNK #1 (BUD). THAT GUTENBERG!

GUTENBERG (DOUG). I prefer Johann!

BOOTBLACK (BUD).
GUTENBERG!

GUTENBERG (DOUG). Hey! It's the Bootblack!

BOOTBLACK (BUD).
SHINE YOUR BOOT-ENBERG?

GUTENBERG (DOUG). Sure, Bootblack.

BOOTBLACK (BUD).
YOU'RE A MAN IN YOUR PRIME
MAKING FRIENDS ALL THE TIME
NO REFUTIN'-BERG!

(*Asking for payment.*) Ten ducats.

GUTENBERG (DOUG). Hey! Hey! Hey!

(**GUTENBERG** *flips a coin in the air to* **BOOTBLACK.**)

BOOTBLACK (BUD). Yeah, Gutenberg! Ho Ho Ho!

GUTENBERG (DOUG). Okay now fellas, I've got to be getting back to my wine press shop. Don't you guys have anything to do?

DRUNK #1 (BUD). No!

DRUNK #2 (DOUG). It's not like we can read.

BOOTBLACK (BUD). *(Picking a fight with* **DRUNK #2**.*) You* can't read!

DRUNK #2 (DOUG). *You* can't read!

BOOTBLACK (BUD). Why I – Shut up!

> *(They start to fist fight and* **GUTENBERG** *gets between them.)*

GUTENBERG (DOUG). Hey! …Let's not fight.

> *(They fight some more.)*

Why don't I buy you a flower from that adorable little flower girl?

LI'L NAZI GIRL (BUD).

> HERE'S A PRETTY POSEY, IT'S THE FIRST ONE OF THE SPRING

> *(Then, as an aside.)*

> I STOLE IT FROM A JEW!
> MY HEART IS FULL OF HATE, AND I DON'T KNOW ANYTHING
> 'CAUSE YES, I'M ILLITERATE TOO!

> *(***GUTENBERG** *hasn't heard any of the aside. He spins into a spotlight.)*

GUTENBERG (DOUG).

> OOOOH!
> SCHLIMMER!
> MY LOVELY SCHLIMMER!
> YOU ARE THE BEST DARN TOWN IN GERMANY!

> *(The* **CAST** *criss-cross the stage.)*

BOOTBLACK (BUD).
 GUTENBERG!

  BEEF FAT TRIMMER (DOUG).
  GUTENBERG!

   LI'L NAZI GIRL (BUD).
   GUTENBERG!

    DRUNKS 1 & 2 (BUD & DOUG).
    GUTENBER-GUH!

  *(**BUD** and **DOUG** regroup in a quick huddle to re-set the hats for the ending saying things like "Big finish! Big finish!" When they emerge, **DOUG** wears the **GUTENBERG** hat. **BUD** holds the rest and at the appropriate time, he puppets them to look like a group singing behind **GUTENBERG**.)*

GUTENBERG (DOUG).
 I'M THE PRIDE OF
  SCHLIMMER
 I'M THE CREME DE LA
  CREMMER
 I'M THE PRIDE OF
  SCHLIMMER
 I'M THE CREME DE LA
  CREMMER
 I'M GU-TEN-BERG!

EVERYONE ELSE (BUD).
 HE'S THE PRIDE OF
  SCHLIMMER
 HE'S THE CREME DE LA
  CREMMER
 HE'S THE PRIDE OF
  SCHLIMMER
 HE'S GU-OO-TEN-BERG!

  *(After applause, **BUD** and **DOUG** address the audience:)*

DOUG. That was the opening number.

BUD. *(He's proud of both.)* And the prologue.

DOUG. We're just trying to give you a sense of the world of Schlimmer!

BUD. It's a tiny town!

DOUG. Very tiny. The kind of town you might hear about on a podcast or a Netflix documentary.

BUD. True crime!

DOUG. Yes! The kind of town where everyone's friendly... but also suspicious. So you might hear something like this:

> *(They begin a very well-rehearsed, broadly-played scene.)*

BUD. "Well, if it isn't my good friend, Doug Simon, stopping by for a shave and a haircut."

DOUG. "I sure am, barber. Hey barber! I brought you a gift. It's a cupcake."

> *(He pretends to give* **BUD** *a cupcake.)*

BUD. "Why, Thank you."

> *(He pretends to eat it.)*

"This cupcake is poison!"

DOUG. *(Distraught melodrama.)* "I can't stop killing!"

> *(***BUD** *and* **DOUG** *bow.)*

So as you can see, Schlimmer's the kind of town where anything can happen. And now we start the story. *(Stage direction.)* Scene Two:

[MUSIC NO. 2A – SCENE 2 UNDERSCORE]

Gutenberg's Wine Press Shop. The roof is made of dirty thatch. There are shelves filled with old wine bottles. And we meet Helvetica, a German girl who's beautiful but does not know it. She stands in a bucket stomping on grapes. Gutenberg enters.

> *(***BUD**, *as* **HELVETICA**, *stands in the box labeled "BUCKET."* **DOUG**, *as* **GUTENBERG**, *stalks the stage.)*

HELVETICA (BUD). Gutenberg!

GUTENBERG (DOUG). Hello! Man, I love this town.

HELVETICA (BUD). I love *you*.

[MUSIC NO. 2B – HELVETICA INTRO]

(Musical interlude. They lock eyes. **DOUG** *breaks it to address the audience:)*

DOUG. *(Stage direction.)* There is an extremely awkward pause.

*(***DOUG*** *returns to the stare with* **BUD,** *holds for the pause, then continues suddenly.)*

GUTENBERG (DOUG). Have you seen my dream journal? I had an amazing dream last night and I want to turn it into a poem.

HELVETICA (BUD). A poem! Will you read it to me?

GUTENBERG (DOUG). Journals are private.

HELVETICA (BUD). Yes sir.

GUTENBERG (DOUG). Oh! I almost forgot. Here's a flower.

HELVETICA (BUD). It's beautiful!

(She takes it and adores it.)

GUTENBERG (DOUG). I got it from that horrible anti-semitic flower girl. Destroy it.

HELVETICA (BUD). Yes sir.

(She does.)

GUTENBERG (DOUG). There will be no hatred in my shop.

HELVETICA (BUD). Are you hungry?

GUTENBERG (DOUG). Yes.

HELVETICA (BUD). Do you want me to bake a lamb for you?

GUTENBERG (DOUG). No. But I would like some stew.

HELVETICA (BUD). Lamb stew? Right away, sir.

GUTENBERG (DOUG). Good girl. I love ewe!

HELVETICA (BUD). You love me!

> (**DOUG** *plays the following pun as a tragic misunderstanding.)*

GUTENBERG (DOUG). No. I love ewe. E-W-E. Ewe.

HELVETICA (BUD). E-W-Who?

GUTENBERG (DOUG). Ewe!

HELVETICA (BUD). Me?

GUTENBERG (DOUG). Stew! Female Lamb Stew!

HELVETICA (BUD). I don't understand!

GUTENBERG (DOUG). WHY CAN NO ONE IN THIS TOWN READ?!?!?!

HELVETICA (BUD). We have nothing to read.

[MUSIC NO. 2C – NOTHING TO READ]

GUTENBERG (DOUG). I see. *That* is the problem. I'll be in my wine press room. Pressing wine.

HELVETICA (BUD). Here's your stew. I made it, hot and ready.

GUTENBERG (DOUG). Thank you, um…Barbara.

HELVETICA (BUD). Helvetica.

GUTENBERG (DOUG). Helvetica! Yes. Thank you. You know… I couldn't make it without you. The wine, I mean.

[MUSIC NO. 3 – I CAN'T READ]

HELVETICA (BUD). Yes sir. Thank you sir. Wonderful sir.

(As **HELVETICA** *sings, we see* **GUTENBERG**
*working at his press in slow motion. The
press is a box labeled "Wine Press" – sitting
on a stool.*)

HELVETICA (BUD).
I WATCH HIM WORKING AT HIS PRESS
I WATCH HIM MAKE HIS WINE
I STOMP THE GRAPES
AND DREAM ABOUT
THE DAY I'LL MAKE HIM MINE
BUT I KNOW THAT DAY WILL NEVER COME
'CAUSE I AM TOO OBTUSE
I'M JUST TOO DUMB TO UNDERSTAND
ANYTHING BUT THIS GRAPE JUICE

AND I
I CAN'T READ
I CAN'T READ HIM
HE'S ALL GREEK TO ME

BUT I...
I, I, I
I STILL NEED HIM
LIKE A GRAPE THAT NEEDS A SQUEEZE

HIS BRAIN IS BIGGER THAN MY BRAIN
HE CAN SPELL AND COUNT REAL GOOD
AND ME? WHY I DON'T COUNT AT ALL
AND I DON'T THINK I SHOULD

'CAUSE I WAS RAISED TO MILK A COW
AND SIT UPON A STOOL
AND COWS THEY NEVER ASK YOU MUCH
NO WONDER I'M A FOOL!
ALSO, THERE'S NO SCHOOL!

AND I
I AM DUMB
I AM DUMBSTRUCK

EV'RY TIME HE SAYS MY NAME:
HEL-
VE-TI-CA
GUMMISTIEFEL
HELVETICA GUMMISTIEFEL

> (**GUTENBERG** *fades away, leaving only* **HELVETICA** *on stage.*)

GUMMISTIEFEL
IT'S BEEN MY NAME SINCE BIRTH
BUT THERE'S ONE NAME I'D TRADE IT FOR
ON THIS FLAT PLANET EARTH
SO I'LL STAY HERE IN MY BUCKET
AND ONE DAY I'LL BE
HELVETICA GUTENBERG
JUST YOU WAIT AND SEE!

I
I'LL BE HERE
I'LL BE HEARING CHURCH BELLS
CHURCH BELLS FOR US
AND US
US OR WE?
BE TOGETHER
WHICHEVER: US OR WE
US OR WE!
US OR WE!
US OR WE!
(Spoken in rhythm.) US OR WE!

> (*After applause,* **BUD** *and* **DOUG** *address the audience:*)

DOUG. Wow.

BUD. Thank you. Always a very emotional moment for me, that song.

DOUG. *(Genuine.)* You nailed it, buddy.

DOUG. *(Then, to the audience.)* The first time I heard Bud sing that song, we were in a TGIFridays. They brought us a free dessert.

BUD. I'm lactose intolerant!

DOUG. Anyway, that was the love ballad.

BUD. But Doug, what is a love ballad?

DOUG. Well people like me and Bud call a song like that the "I Want" song because Helvetica wants Gutenberg.

BUD. But the real question is – does Gutenberg know that?

DOUG. I don't think so.

BUD. How could he not?

(A quick look between them, then –)

DOUG. Now, you're probably sitting there and thinking to yourself "Did Helvetica actually exist?"

BUD. Hmm... Probably!

DOUG. Yes! "History" tells us that in olden times there were a lot of poor wenches, so chances are, if Helvetica did exist, Gutenberg probably knew her.

BUD. Also – her name is a font!

DOUG. Yes. These days, we don't name fonts after anybody.

BUD. Not even Beyoncé.

DOUG. Beyoncé would be a fierce font. But now it's time to meet the bad guys! The Town Monk and his henchman Young Monk.

BUD. Watch out!

DOUG. *(Stage directions.)* Scene Three:

[MUSIC NO. 3A – SCENE 3 UNDERSCORE]

The Church on the Hill. The roof is made of dirty thatch. In the corner there's a giant Bible. On this wall, there's a velvet painting of Jesus crying. Monk, an evil man who hates God –

>   (**MONK (BUD)** *flips off God.*)

– is sitting at his desk, sharpening a pencil.

>   (**MONK** *sharpens his pencil – it is an electric pencil sharpener.*)

He is very good at it.

>   (**MONK** *sharpens again.*)

BUD. His henchman, Young Monk, enters.

>   (*NOTE: The cat in the following is VERY realistic-looking – more like bad taxidermy than a toy – that's treated throughout as alive.*)

YOUNG MONK (DOUG). *(Holding the cat.)* Monk! Look, I found a cat in the alley.

MONK (BUD). Give him to me!

>   (**YOUNG MONK** *hands him the cat.* **MONK** *pets it.*)

Oh. Pretty kitty. I shall name you…Satan.

>   (*During this,* **YOUNG MONK** *has moved to the big Bible.*)

Young Monk! What are you doing over there by that Bible?

YOUNG MONK (DOUG). Teaching myself how to read.

(He reads, haltingly.) "In… the… be-jinning –"

MONK (BUD). Get him, Satan!

>   (**MONK** *throws the cat at* **YOUNG MONK**. *It attacks him.* **YOUNG MONK** *thrashes violently and painfully.*)

MONK (BUD). You see what happens when you try to learn to read, Young Monk?!

> *(The cat springs back into* **MONK***'s hands. He pets it.)*

Now let's try this again. What are you doing over there by that Bible?

YOUNG MONK (DOUG). Nothing.

MONK (BUD). *(Petting the cat.)* That's right.

> As long as I'm the Monk, no one in this town is going to learn to read. That way, the Bible says whatever I says it says. Unless, of course,

[MUSIC NO. 3B – UNLESS OF COURSE UNDERSCORE]

someone... *(As the speech intensifies, the petting becomes violent.)* ...were to make a machine...that prints books...and then printed up a mess of copies of the Bible...and distributed them to the masses.

YOUNG MONK (DOUG). You're hurting Satan!

MONK (BUD). Oh no! No! I don't want to hurt Satan, I *love* Satan. *(He nuzzles the cat.)* Yes I do! Yes I do! *(Out to the audience.)* I love Satan.

[MUSIC NO. 4 – HAUNTED GERMAN WOOD]

YOUNG MONK (DOUG). You're such a bad Monk.

MONK (BUD). Yes. Yes, I am.

> WHEN I WAS A YOUNG MONK
> I TRIED TO FEED THE POOR
> I PRAYED TO JESUS, I HELPED THE LAME
> BUT I ALWAYS WANTED MORE
> GOD SAID, "BE MEEK AND BE WEAK AND BE GOOD"

YOUNG MONK (DOUG).

> GOOD!

MONK (BUD).
>BUT THEN I MET THE DEVIL
>IN A HAUNTED GERMAN WOOD

YOUNG MONK (DOUG). So...you met the actual devil...in a forest?

MONK (BUD). Uh huh!

>THE DEVIL WAS A LADY
>HE LOOKED JUST LIKE MY MOM
>HE HELD ME LIKE A BABY
>AND LIKE A BABY I SUCKED MY THUMB
>HE SAID, "YOU'RE SO SMALL, I CAN MAKE YOU A MAN!"

YOUNG MONK (DOUG).
>MAN!

MONK (BUD). *(Spoken in rhythm.)*
>THEN HE THREW ME IN THE DIRT!
>AND HE SLAPPED ME WITH BOTH HANDS!

(**MONK & YOUNG MONK** *dance together.)*

MONK & YOUNG MONK (BUD & DOUG).
>HAUNTED GERMAN WOOD
>HAUNTED GERMAN WOOD

MONK (BUD). *(Spoken in rhythm.)*
>I SOLD MY SOUL FOR POWER!

MONK & YOUNG MONK (BUD & DOUG).
>IN A HAUNTED GERMAN WOOD

YOUNG MONK (DOUG).
>THIS SEEMS BAD!

MONK (BUD).
>IT'S NOT BAD
>JUST A DANCE WITH THE DEVIL

MONK (BUD).	**YOUNG MONK (DOUG).**
I WORSHIP SATAN!	YOU WORSHIP SATAN!

MONK (BUD).

> THE DEVIL SAID HE HAD TO GO
> BACK WHERE HE'D COME FROM
> BUT HE TOLD ME, "BOY, STAY IN THE CHURCH
> AND KEEP THE PEOPLE DUMB.
> THEY WON'T SUSPECT YOU IF THEY THINK YOU'RE

MONK & YOUNG MONK (BUD & DOUG).

> GOOD!

MONK (BUD). *(Spoken in rhythm.)*

> BUT THERE'S GONNA COME A DAY
> WHEN A GUY WILL PRINT A BOOK
> AND THE BOOK WILL BE THE BIBLE
> AND THE PEOPLE ALL WILL READ IT
> AND THEY'LL KNOW THAT YOU'RE A LIAR
> SO YOU'RE GONNA HAVE TO STOP HIM

> > (**MONK** *stops –* **BUD** *uses his inhaler. Then* **MONK** *adds –)*

> 'CAUSE IF YOU DON'T THEN WE JUST WASTED
> LIKE, AN AWFUL LOT OF TIME
> IN THIS HAUNTED GERMAN WOOD

MONK & YOUNG MONK (BUD & DOUG).

> HAUNTED GERMAN WOOD
> HAUNTED GERMAN WOOD

MONK (BUD).

YOU'RE HAUNTED	**YOUNG MONK (DOUG).**
	AND YOU'RE GERMAN
YOU HAUNTED	
	GERMAN
HAUNTED GERMAN	HAUNTED GERMAN
HAUNTED GERMAN	
WOOD	HAUNTED GERMAN
HAUNTED GERMAN	WOOD
WOOD	HAUNTED GERMAN

MONK (BUD).
> NOW IT IS THE DEVIL'S TURN!
> I SEE A BOOK – I'LL HAVE IT BURNED!
> I'LL ALWAYS TREASURE WHAT I LEARNED
> IN THAT HAUNTED GERMAN

> > (**MONK** *throws the pencil at* **YOUNG MONK**. *It embeds itself in his chest like an arrow. He screams and falls, injured.*)

MONK (BUD). Yah!

YOUNG MONK (DOUG). Owww!

MONK & YOUNG MONK (BUD & DOUG).
> WOOD!

> > (NOTE: *The pencil stabbing is accomplished through a simple stage trick.* **BUD** *pretends to throw a pencil.* **DOUG** *has a pencil hidden in his pocket and pulls it out and holds it to his chest to make it look like* **MONK**'s *pencil has flown across the room and stabbed him in the chest.*)

> > (*After applause,* **BUD** *and* **DOUG** *address the audience:*)

DOUG. Now that is a bad monk!

BUD. In his defense, he was tricked by the devil.

DOUG. Yes. A lot of us get tricked by the devil.

BUD. My dad got tricked by the devil. He cheated on my mom with a bank teller.

DOUG. A very pretty bank teller.

BUD. Yes. My parents are still together though!

DOUG. Marriage! Now – we hate Monk. And we hope you do too. But we want you to hate him for a reason.

BUD. Yes! You can't just say a character is evil. You've got to know why he's evil.

DOUG. That's why we had him worship Satan.

BUD. It's called character development. Now – I think I heard the Monk saying something about how he doesn't want a person to make a machine that prints books.

DOUG. Uh-oh! 'Cause guess who's about to make a machine that prints books!! *(Stage direction.)* Scene Four:

[MUSIC NO. 5 – THE PRESS]

BUD. *(Stage direction.)* Gutenberg's Wine Press Shop. It is very late at night. The clock on the wall says, like, two a.m. probably. Gutenberg is working at his press.

GUTENBERG (DOUG). Ah! I need a break!

WHEN I'M AT MY PRESS
I LIKE TO LEAVE MY BODY
LET MY MIND ROAM FREE
AND THINK ABOUT MY DAY

SOMEBODY DIED
SOMEBODY CRIED
SOMEBODY LIED
I ATE STEW

AND YET
THERE'S THE PAIN OF SOMETHING
NIGGLING AT MY HEAD
I CAN'T FORGET
AND YET I CAN'T REMEMBER
WHAT THE PEOPLE OF SCHLIMMER SAID

BOOTBLACK (BUD).
I CANNOT READ!

DAUGHTER (BUD).
I CANNOT READ!

DRUNK #1 (BUD).
I CANNOT READ!

LI'L NAZI GIRL (BUD).
I HATE JEWS!

GUTENBERG (DOUG). Yes! I hear you now, Townspeople! And I understand you! I feel you inside me! *(A moment of realization.)* And I've got to do something.

HERE! I'LL TAKE THIS CLOCK
WHAT CAN THIS BE?
CAN THIS CLOCK EVER TEACH PEOPLE TO READ?

NO IT CANNOT.
IT GOES IN THE TRASH
WAIT! THERE MIGHT BE SOMETHING COOL IN THE TRASH!

IT'S JUST AN OLD GRAPE
THAT'S NOT WHAT I NEED
GRAPES ARE COMPLETELY USELESS

NO! SCHLIMMER MUST READ!
BUT WHAT CAN I DO?
ALL I'VE GOT'S THIS GRAPE JUICE PRESS

Wait a minute...

THIS GRAPE JUICE...
...PRESS.

> (**GUTENBERG** *starts to work on the printing press.)*

I'M GONNA TAKE THIS PRESS
AND MAKE IT PRINT SOME WORDS
I'M GONNA CHANGE THIS PRESS
THOUGH I KNOW IT SOUNDS ABSURD

I'M GONNA TAKE THE GRAPES OUT
AND PUT LETTERS IN
PUT LETTERS WHERE THEM GRAPES HAVE BEEN
GONNA CHANGE THIS PRESS
AND MAKE IT PRINT SOME WORDS

OLD NARRATOR (BUD). *(Folksy old man.)* And so Gutenberg worked long into the night, making history to a boogie-woogie beat. You go on there, Johann Gutenberg! You invent that printing press for all of us!

> *(**OLD NARRATOR** and **GUTENBERG** high five.)*

> *(As **GUTENBERG** sings the following lines, he completes the simple transformation of the Wine Press to the Printing Press. This transformation should be as simple as changing a sign.)*

GUTENBERG (DOUG).
> IT'S THE FIRST PRINTING PRESS IN HISTORY
> IT'S GONNA PRINT-UP BOOKS FOR YOU AND ME
> IT'S A PRINTING PRESS
> AND IT'S GONNA PRINT SOME WORDS

DOUG. *(Stage direction.)* Helvetica enters.

HELVETICA (BUD). Gutenberg!

GUTENBERG (DOUG). Look what I invented!

> *(He motions to the new printing press.)*

HELVETICA (BUD). What is it?

GUTENBERG (DOUG). A printing press!

HELVETICA (BUD). It's wonderful! Should we toast?

> *(**HELVETICA** mimes a wine glass.)*

GUTENBERG (DOUG). No!

> *(**GUTENBERG** knocks the glass out of her hand and shatters it. Music out.)*

Silly girl! We don't make wine anymore. Now, we make words!

HELVETICA (BUD). Words?!

> (**GUTENBERG** *pushes her out of his way.*)

GUTENBERG (DOUG). Words!
AH! NOW THAT I'M DONE
GET READY TO READ!
THIS WILL BE GOING DOWN IN HISTORY

REMEMBER MY FACE!
NOW THERE'S A GLIMMER IN SCHLIMMER...
AND THAT GLIMMER IS ME!
G-U-T-E-N-B-E-R-G!
(Spoken in rhythm.) YEAH!

> (*After applause,* **BUD** *and* **DOUG** *address the audience:*)

DOUG. History!

BUD. I'd just like to say, it was pretty scary setting the most important moment in history to music.

DOUG. Well, you did a great job.

BUD. Well, you wrote me a great story.

> (*Beat of mutual admiration.* **DOUG** *is overwhelmed and goes "off-script.")*

DOUG. *(To* **BUD.***)* This is awesome!

BUD. *(To* **DOUG.***)* We're doing it!

DOUG. I just want to say – I'm gonna go off-script for a second.

BUD. Do it. Go off-script.

DOUG. *(To the audience.)* I'm going off script. I just want to say that when I'm singing that song, I'm singing about this giant moment for Gutenberg, but I'm thinking about – *(To* **BUD.***)* Do you know what I'm thinking about?

BUD. I have no idea and I don't want to guess.

DOUG. The day of our miracle!

BUD. Miracle –? Oh boy, that's not –

DOUG. *(To audience.)* Bud brought a dead lady back to life.

BUD. Oh no, I didn't.

DOUG. He did! Here's the story – Bud and I used to work at a nursing home.

BUD. We still do.

DOUG. Yes. But we used to do these lip sync concerts for people in wheelchairs.

BUD. They are such a great audience.

DOUG. It's mostly the classics – ya know, Frank Sinatra, James Brown, Cynthia Lauper –

BUD. But we take requests!

DOUG. Yes! And one day, from the back of the room, this poker named Fran McCallister –

BUD. Wait, Doug, they don't know what a poker is, you have to tell them.

DOUG. Oh, right – In nursing home lingo, we call someone a "poker" if you have to "poke her" to make sure she's still alive.

BUD. Fran McCallister was our oldest poker.

DOUG. She had not said a single word in over a *year*. She just sat there in her wheelchair, grippin' those arms with her face frozen like GRRRRRRR –

BUD. She was praying for death.

DOUG. Oh, clearly. So – there we are, asking for requests when suddenly, out of nowhere, comes this voice that sounds like it's from the pit of hell –

BUD. "DOOOON'T CRYYYYY FRENCHY!"

DOUG. It was Fran McCallister!

BUD. I thought she was possessed by the devil.

DOUG. I still think she might have been. But she was requesting a song, so I looked up "Don't Cry Frenchy" and...it's from World War *One*.

BUD. The original.

DOUG. Now, of course, we didn't have a lip-sync track for "Don't Cry Frenchy." And even if we did –

BUD. It was probably racist.

DOUG. Yes. Most old songs are racist. So – there I am, about to tell this woman who *never* talks, and has no hope left, that we are not going to be able to lip-sync to her favorite ancient racist song when Bud, outta nowhere, starts *singing* –

BUD. I don't know what it was. Something came over me.

DOUG. He *made up* a song! Out of *nothing*. He just made it up! Sing it, Bud. Just like you did that day. You be you and I'll be Fran McAllister.

> (**DOUG** *sits and acts out being immobilized in a wheelchair as* **BUD** *sings – to the tune of "We Eat Dreams" – "Where our little lives," etc.)*

[MUSIC NO. 5A – DON'T CRY FRENCHY]

BUD.

PLEASE DON'T CRY MY LITTLE FRENCHY,
PLEASE DON'T CRY
DON'T YOU WORRY, LITTLE FRENCHY,
YOU WON'T DIE
WELL NOT TODAY

(As **BUD** *sings,* **DOUG** *– as old Fran McAllister – dramatically starts to move, then to clap and then he stands, clapping –!)*

BUD.
'CAUSE WE'RE HERE FROM THE U-S-A!

*(***DOUG** *– still as Fran – applauds wildly. Then, he turns to the audience, excited –)*

DOUG. She *stood up*! Out of her wheelchair! Bud *healed* her! His music healed her!

BUD. Briefly.

DOUG. Yes, she died two days later, but she died *happy*. And it was all 'cause of Bud.

BUD. No.

DOUG. Yes! It wasn't even the song she asked for! It was something new – something she wanted and she didn't even know it yet. That's what made it a miracle.

BUD. It wasn't a miracle.

DOUG. Well it was a miracle for me, 'cause when Bud made up that song – I knew right then and there that things were gonna change. And not just change – they were gonna get better. For both of us.

BUD. And hey…look at us now. We wrote a musical! Even Johann Gutenberg couldn't do that.

DOUG. *(Affectionate.)* Well, he never tried…'cause they hadn't invented pianos.

(Then, pivoting out.) Okay, I'm going back on script.

BUD. Do it. Go back on script.

DOUG. Now – you're probably sitting there and thinking to yourself: "Wait a minute, a wine presser invented the printing press?"

BUD. Makes sense! He was already familiar with *pressing* things.

DOUG. *(Question and answer for the audience's benefit.)* What is the difference between a wine press and a printing press? One makes you drink, the other makes you think.

BUD. And that was almost a lyric.

DOUG. I think it should have been.

BUD. Meh. Now, Gutenberg is amazing, but unless I'm crazy, he's not the only character in this show.

DOUG. You're not crazy! *(Stage direction.)* Scene Five: The Streets of Schlimmer.

[MUSIC NO. 6 – I CAN'T READ (REPRISE)]

BUD. *(Stage direction.)* The sky is sad and the air smells like trash. Young Monk is walking in the rain.

> *(***YOUNG MONK (DOUG)*** *still has the pencil sticking out of his chest.* **DOUG** *simply holds it there.* **BUD** *creates rain over his head with a spray bottle.)*

YOUNG MONK (DOUG). *(Walking in place.)*
I'M JUST TOO DUMB TO UNDERSTAND
WHY HE TREATS ME LIKE A DOG
AND LIKE A DOG

I – I CAN'T READ
BUT IF I COULD READ
I COULD GET A DIFF'RENT JOB
WHY CAN'T SOMEONE TEACH ME HOW TO READ?

[MUSIC NO. 6A – BOOTBLACK SHOP UNDERSCORE]

BUD. *(Stage direction.)* Young Monk enters the Bootblack shop.

YOUNG MONK (DOUG). *(Making sound of bell on shop door.)* Dangle, dangle, dangle.

BOOTBLACK (BUD). Young Monk!

YOUNG MONK (DOUG). Hello Bootblack – I got another pencil.

BOOTBLACK (BUD). And I've got a big pair of boot tongs! Allow me to remove it.

> *(He does.* **YOUNG MONK** *screams in ridiculous pain.)*

YOUNG MONK (DOUG). Thank you.

BOOTBLACK (BUD). That's the third pencil this week, Young Monk.

YOUNG MONK (DOUG). I know. Monk has created a hostile workplace environment.

BOOTBLACK (BUD). Then why do you stay with him?

YOUNG MONK (DOUG). I think I can change him.

[MUSIC NO. 6B – YOUNG MONK UNDERSCORE]

He's like a tiny seedling that just needs the water of me. And with a little bit of luck, that me-water will help him grow into a giant tree... *(Starting to cry.)* ...that doesn't stab me with pencils.

> *(He cries harder into* **BOOTBLACK***'s shoulder.)*

BOOTBLACK (BUD). Oh, Young Monk, I know what can cheer you up. Have a biscuit!

[MUSIC NO. 7 – BISCUITS]

> *(***BOOTBLACK** *offers* **YOUNG MONK** *a cookie. He takes it and sings.)*

YOUNG MONK (DOUG).
> BISCUITS!
> BISCUITS!
> I WANT YOU DEEP INSIDE OF ME
> BISCUITS!

BOOTBLACK (BUD). Every medieval bootblack knows, if you're feeling bad, there's only two cures – leeches and biscuits!

YOUNG MONK (DOUG).
> PUT 'EM IN AN OVEN
> AND THEY'RE NICE AND SWEET
> PUT 'EM IN MY TUMMY
> AND THEY'RE GOOD TO EAT
> PUT 'EM ON A SHELF
> AND THEY'RE OUT OF REACH
> BISCUITS!

BOOTBLACK (BUD).
> THEY TASTE REALLY YUMMY
> IN A TIME OF WAR

YOUNG MONK (DOUG).
> TASTE REALLY YUMMY
> EVEN OFF THE FLOOR

BOOTBLACK (BUD).
> TASTE REALLY YUMMY
> AND I WANT SOME MORE

YOUNG MONK & BOOTBLACK (DOUG & BUD).
> WE'RE NOT TOO POOR TO EAT
> BISCUITS!
> BISCUITS!
> I WANT YOU DEEP INSIDE OF ME
> BISCUITS!
> BISCUITS!
> YOU MAKE ME WANT TO DANCE

(They dance...)

YOUNG MONK (DOUG), BOOTBLACK (BUD) & BAND.
(Shouted in rhythm.)
BISCUITS!
BISCUITS!

BOOTBLACK (BUD). And now! I'm going to throw this biscuit into that hat!

> *(He throws a biscuit across the stage into* **YOUNG MONK**'s *hat.)*

YOUNG MONK & BOOTBLACK (DOUG & BUD).
BISCUITS!

YOUNG MONK (DOUG).
YOU CAN EAT A BISCUIT
WHEN YOU'RE SICK IN BED

BOOTBLACK (BUD).
YOU CAN EAT A BISCUIT
WHEN THE MOON TURNS RED

YOUNG MONK (DOUG).
YOU CAN EAT A BISCUIT
WHEN WE'RE ALL DEAD!

YOUNG MONK & BOOTBLACK (DOUG & BUD).
BISCUITS AND BISCUITS AND
BISCUITS!

> *(After applause,* **BUD** *and* **DOUG** *address the audience:)*

DOUG. Now, I know, you're probably sitting there and thinking to yourself, "That song had nothing to do with anything!"

BUD. This show is not about biscuits!

DOUG. So what are we doing? Well, people like me and Bud call a song like that a "Charm Song."

BUD. *(For the audience's benefit – informercial.)* But Doug, why do we need a Charm Song?

DOUG. Well, a Charm Song gives the audience a break from watching the stuff they actually care about.

BUD. Also, a Charm Song can help get a really famous person to play a really tiny part. For instance, we are hoping that one day the role of Young Monk will be played by Mister Timothée Chalamet.

DOUG. And that is not how I thought you pronounced either of those words.

BUD. But enough about biscuits. Gutenberg just invented the printing press! But nobody knows that yet. *(Stage direction.)* Scene Six: The Schlimmer Market! A stinky place full of rotten fruit, dead bodies, and antiques.

[MUSIC NO. 8 – WHAT'S THE WORD]

*(**BUD** and **DOUG** make animal sounds.)*

DOUG. *(Stage direction.)* Rumors about Gutenberg spread like the plague.

(Spoken in rhythm.)

WOMAN (BUD).
HEY, BEEF FAT TRIMMER
SEE YOU'RE CHOPPING SOME MEAT

BEEF FAT TRIMMER (DOUG).
I JUST CAN'T SEEM TO CHOP OFF THESE FEET
FOUR MORE STEAKS AND I'LL HAVE FINISHED THE HERD

WOMAN (BUD).
THEN TAKE A BREAK, AND TELL ME "WHAT'S THE WORD?"

BEEF FAT TRIMMER & WOMAN (DOUG & BUD).
WHAT'S THE WORD?
WHAT'S THE WORD?

BEEF FAT TRIMMER (DOUG).
>WELL, I SHOULDN'T SAY THIS, BUT LATE LAST NIGHT
>IN THE WINE PRESS SHOP THERE WAS A LIGHT
>I SAW GUTENBERG THROUGH THE WINDOW PANE
>HE WAS SWEATING,
>HE WAS WORKING,
>HE WAS SHOUTING HIS NAME
>NOW I WOULDN'T BET MONEY, BUT I THINK IT'S TRUE
>THAT OUR WINE-MAKIN' MAN WAS MAKING SOMETHING
>   NEW

WOMAN (BUD). Really?!

BEEF FAT TRIMMER (DOUG).
>YOU DIDN'T HEAR IT FROM ME.
>I'M JUST A BEEF FAT TRIMMER TRIMMING THE FAT OFF
>   OF BEEF.

BEEF FAT TRIMMER & WOMAN (DOUG & BUD).
>WHAT'S THE WORD?
>WHAT'S THE WORD?

DOUG. *(Stage direction.)*	**WOMAN (BUD).**
Woman goes to buy some cheese.	WHAT'S THE WORD? WHAT'S THE WORD?

WOMAN (BUD).
>WELL, HEY, THERE

ANOTHER WOMAN (DOUG).
>HEY, I'M MILKING A COW

WOMAN (BUD).
>DO YOU REALLY HAVE TO MILK THAT COW RIGHT NOW?
>'CAUSE I GOT HOT GOSSIP AND IT JUST WON'T KEEP
>GUTENBERG DIDN'T GET MUCH SLEEP
>LAST NIGHT

ANOTHER WOMAN (DOUG).
>THAT RIGHT?

WOMAN (BUD).

HE MIGHT BE WORKING ON SOMETHING SHADY
OR HE MIGHT BE WORKING ON A SPECIAL LADY

ANOTHER WOMAN (DOUG).

A SPECIAL LADY! I WISH IT WERE ME!
I'M VERY ATTRACTED TO MISTER G
HE'S GOT GREAT BUNS AND HE'S GOT GREAT PECS
I'LL BE HEARTBROKEN IF HE'S HAVING SEX WITHOUT ME

WOMAN (BUD).

I SEE!

ANOTHER WOMAN (DOUG).

IT CAN'T BE!

ANOTHER WOMAN & WOMAN (DOUG & BUD).

WHAT'S THE WORD?
WHAT'S THE WORD?

ANOTHER WOMAN (DOUG).	**BUD.**	*(Stage direction.)*
WHAT'S THE WORD?	Another Woman sees	
WHAT'S THE WORD?	Friend in a field.	

ANOTHER WOMAN (DOUG).

WELL, HEY!
HAVE YOU HEARD WHAT THEY'RE SAYING, MISTER?
GUTENBERG'S GOT A GIRL
AND HE MIGHT HAVE KISSED HER!
THERE'S JUST ONE PROBLEM – IT WASN'T ME!
SOME OTHER COW IN TOWN'S GIVIN' MILK FOR FREE!
MISTER G'S STEPPIN' OUT WITH SOME PRETTY MISS?
GONNA TELL THE WHOLE TOWN SHE'S GOT SYPHILIS
YOU WANNA GO AND SPREAD THAT RUMOR?

FRIEND OF GUTENBERG (BUD).

MAYBE
BUT FIRST I GOTTA BURY MY DEAD BABY

> *(**BUD** reveals the same **DEAD BABY** hat from the Prologue. He drops it on the ground. A solemn beat.)*

ANOTHER WOMAN (DOUG). That's horrible.

FRIEND OF GUTENBERG (BUD). It happens.

FRIEND OF GUTENBERG & ANOTHER WOMAN (BUD & DOUG).
WHAT'S THE WORD?
WHAT'S THE WORD?

> *(As* **BUD** *crosses downstage, he hands off the* **FRIEND** *hat to* **DOUG**. **DOUG** *puts it on.)*

FRIEND (DOUG).	**BUD**. *(Stage direction.)*
WHAT'S THE WORD?	A man is buying some
WHAT'S THE WORD?	apricots.

FRIEND OF GUTENBERG (DOUG).
HEY THERE, MAN! I SEE YOU'RE BUYING SOME FRUIT.
HAVE YOU HEARD THE NEWS ABOUT OUR FRIEND
   GUTENBERG?
IT SEEMS HE'S DONE SOMETHING GREAT.
BUT ALL WE KNOW FOR CERTAIN IS HE WAS UP LATE!

> *(The man spins around – it's* **MONK***!)*

It's Monk!

MONK (BUD).
SAY NO MORE, MY CHILDLESS FRIEND
I'LL FIND OUT WHERE THIS RUMOR ENDS
I'LL HEAD ON OVER TO THE WINE PRESS SHOP
AND IF HE'S UP TO SOMETHING NAUGHTY –
I'LL MAKE IT STOP!

MONK & EVERYONE (BUD & DOUG). *(Ad lib.)* Secrets!
Whispers and secrets! Whispers and secrets!

> *(After applause,* **BUD** *and* **DOUG** *address the audience:)*

BUD. Wow, wasn't it nice to catch-up with all of our townspeople again?

DOUG. It sure was, Bud. You see, this show has a huge cast –

BUD. Huge.

DOUG. – and when a musical has that many actors backstage, you need to use them or they get cranky.

BUD. And speaking of cranky, it looks like Monk's headed over to the wine press shop to see what Gutenberg's been up to. And just like old wine, the plot...thickens.

(Stage direction.) Scene Seven: Gutenberg's Wine Press Shop.

DOUG. *(Stage direction.)* Helvetica is crying in her bucket.

BUD. *(Stage direction.)* Monk enters.

[MUSIC NO. 8A – WINE PRESS SHOP UNDERSCORE]

MONK (BUD). Knock knock knock. Anybody home?

HELVETICA (DOUG). This is not a home!

(She cries even more.)

MONK (BUD). I'm just here to pick up some wine. Church wine. For the church.

HELVETICA (DOUG). We don't make wine. Not anymore.

MONK (BUD). Ah! You must be Helvetica.

HELVETICA (DOUG). How do you know my name?

MONK (BUD). I'm a Monk, I know everything!

HELVETICA (DOUG). Everything?

MONK (BUD). Everything!

HELVETICA (DOUG). So, you know that I love Gutenberg?

MONK (BUD). No, I did not know that. Until now! And now I know everything!

HELVETICA (DOUG). So you know Gutenberg invented the printing press?

MONK (BUD). What?! NO! Who invented the printing press?

> (**DOUG** *breaks character and sells this to the*
> *audience to make sure they get it.*)

HELVETICA (DOUG). Johann Gutenberg.

MONK (BUD). Johann Gutenberg invented the printing press. What year is this?

HELVETICA (DOUG). *(Still out of character.)* 1450.

MONK (BUD). Johann Gutenberg invented the printing press in the year 1450.

HELVETICA (DOUG). *(Jumping back into character.)* Yes! And it's right there!

[MUSIC NO. 8B – IT'S RIGHT OVER THERE]

MONK (BUD). Well, we'll just see about that.

> (**MONK** *pulls the sheet off the press – and*
> *reacts in horror, like a vampire in the sun.*)

Waa! It burns!

> (*He puts the sheet back. He repeats the reveal/*
> *hide move ad lib.*)

You know what I think, Helvetica?

HELVETICA (DOUG). No.

MONK (BUD). I think you're going to destroy this printing press.

HELVETICA (DOUG). Why?

MONK (BUD). Because – if you don't make wine anymore, what use does Gutenberg have for you?

HELVETICA (DOUG). I don't know.

[MUSIC NO. 9 – STOP THE PRESS]

MONK (BUD). Poor, poor Helvetica...

> YOU'VE MADE WINE
> PROB'LY 'BOUT A MILLION TIMES
> YOU DUMB GERMAN WENCH
> YOU FOOL!
> HE'S GONE
> WHAT IS THAT YOU'RE STOMPIN' ON?
> LET ME TAKE A GUESS
> THERE'S GRAPE JUICE ON YOUR DRESS
> ISN'T IT TIME TO STOP THE PRESS?

HELVETICA (DOUG). You mean destroy his printing press?

MONK (BUD). That's right Helvetica. The only thing standing between you and Gutenberg is that there printing press.

> STOP THE PRESS
> YOU GOTTA STOP THE PRESS
> OR THE PRESS'LL STOP YOU
> STOP THE PRESS
> YOU CAN GET HIM BACK IF YOU GIVE IT A CHOP
>
> YOU STOMPED HIS GRAPES FOR WINE
> NOW STOMP FOR MONK THIS TIME
> YOU'VE GOT TO STOP THE –

HELVETICA (DOUG).

> PLEASE, DON'T SHOUT
> I'M IN THIS BUCKET, I'LL GET OUT
> IF I SMASH HIS PRESS
> HE'LL CRY
> AND I...

MONK (BUD).

> ...WILL BE RIGHT THERE TO DRY HIS EYES

HELVETICA (DOUG).

> I'LL FEEL HIS CARESS

MONK (BUD).
YES!

HELVETICA (DOUG).
WE'LL BE TOGETHER

MONK (BUD).
YES!

HELVETICA (DOUG).
MAYBE IT'S TIME TO STOP THE PRESS!

MONK (BUD). *(Pulling out his pencil.)*
STOP THE PRESS
YOU CAN STOP THE PRESS WITH A SIMPLE PENCIL
STOP THE PRESS

(He makes her take the pencil.)

HELVETICA (DOUG).
I KNOW I'M GONNA DO IT BUT I'M FEELING TENSE
WILL GUTENBERG BE MAD?

MONK (BUD).
NO.

HELVETICA (DOUG).
WILL GUTENBERG BE GLAD?

MONK (BUD).
SURE!

HELVETICA (DOUG).
I'VE GOT TO STOP THE –

MONK (BUD).
PRESS!!!

MONK (BUD).   **HELVETICA (DOUG).**
STOP THE PRESS!   OK, I'LL DO IT

STOP THE PRESS!
                                                     I KNOW I CAN

MONK (BUD).

STOP THE PRESS!

STOP THE PRESS!

USE THAT PENCIL!

YOU'LL BE TOGETHER.

YOU'LL HAVE A BABY!

JOHANN JUNIOR!

HELVETICA (DOUG).

PLEASE DON'T RUSH ME

I LOVE MY MAN!

STOP THE PRESS!

STOP THE PRESS!

STOP THE PRESS!

STOP THE PRESS!

MONK (BUD).

YOU'VE GOT TO STOP THE –

HELVETICA (DOUG).

I LOVE YOU, GUTENBERG!

MONK (BUD).

YOU'VE GOT TO STOP THE –

HELVETICA (DOUG).

THIS IS FOR OUR FUTURE!

MONK (BUD).

YOU'VE GOT TO STOP THE PRESS!!!

> (**HELVETICA** *chops ferociously. The printing press is destroyed.* **BUD** *changes the sign on the box from "PRINTING PRESS" to "RUBBLE."*)

> (**HELVETICA** *sees the rubble and realizes she made a mistake.*)

HELVETICA (DOUG). What have I done?!

MONK (BUD). My bidding!!!!

(After applause, **BUD** *and* **DOUG** *address the audience:)*

DOUG. Holy shit! What the fuck was that?!

BUD. *(To* **DOUG**.*)* Doug! Language!

DOUG. I'm sorry, but Monk and Helvetica just destroyed the printing press! Think about that for a second.

BUD. Let me say something. "History" does not always happen like we think.

DOUG. "History" is not always like they say in the so-called "History Books." Also, this may not have happened.

BUD. But it could have!

DOUG. Yes. You see, we realized – once Gutenberg invented the printing press, there was no more story.

BUD. So we destroyed it!

DOUG. Now anything can happen!

BUD. And what's about to happen is the big Act One finale! Now as many of you already know, a hit Broadway musical has to end its first act with a soaring anthem that tween girls will eventually struggle to sing in the shower.

DOUG. That's why we're about to send you rocking to the restroom.

[MUSIC NO. 10 – TOMORROW IS TONIGHT]

BUD. Elderly patrons may wish to turn down their hearing devices.

DOUG. In an actual production this song would include a gospel choir and lasers.

BUD. *(Stage direction.)* Scene Eight: Rooftops of Schlimmer! Gutenberg stands, straddling a chimney. Smoke billows up around his face.

(In a spotlight – stage right –)

GUTENBERG (DOUG).
WHEN I GOT OUT OF BED TODAY
HISTORY WAS A LOT MORE BORING
THEN I THOUGHT IN A DIFF'RENT WAY
NOW THE BIRD OF INSPIRATION'S SOARING

LOOK AT THESE HANDS
THEY'RE ATTACHED TO A NORMAL MAN
A NORMAL MAN
WHO PROB'LY CHANGED YOUR WORLD!

TOMORROW IS TONIGHT
IT'S A HISTORY AND FUTURE FIGHT!
TOMORROW IS TONIGHT!

DOUG. *(Stage direction.)* Monk rises from an adjacent chimney. He is surrounded by fire and bats.

(In a spotlight – stage left –)

MONK (BUD).
TODAY I KILLED THE FUTURE
NOW MY BADNESS KNOWS NO BOUNDS
MY PLAN UNFURLED
TO TRICK THAT GIRL
NOW THE BIRD OF INSPIRATION'S ON THE GROUND

(Spoken in rhythm.) SPLAT! HAH!

I CRUSHED HIS DREAM
YOU DON'T CHANGE THE WORLD
WITH A DUMB MACHINE
AT LEAST NOT WHILE THIS MONK IS STILL IN TOWN!

TOMORROW IS TONIGHT
IT'S A HISTORY AND FUTURE FIGHT!
TOMORROW IS TONIGHT

BUD. *(Stage direction.)* Helvetica is also on a roof.

*(**DOUG** sits on a stool in a spotlight – center –)*

HELVETICA (DOUG).

I FEEL LIKE A BIRD
A BIRD WHO JUST DESTROYED A PRINTING PRESS
A BIRD WHO'S IN SOME SERIOUS DISTRESS
I DON'T HAVE WINGS
THAT IS BAD FOR FLYING THINGS

> (**DOUG** *leaves the* **HELVETICA** *hat on the stool and moves back to his earlier position to play* **GUTENBERG.** *Individual spotlights hit* **MONK, GUTENBERG,** *and* **HELVETICA** *in a triangle formation –* **HELVETICA** *center.*)

MONK (BUD).

MONK'S IN COMMAND!

GUTENBERG (DOUG).

DON'T SAY CAN'T WHEN YOU COULD SAY CAN!

MONK, HELVETICA & GUTENBERG (BUD & DOUG).

YOU ONLY GET ONE CHANCE TO BE A STAR!
TOMORROW IS TONIGHT
IT'S A HISTORY AND FUTURE FIGHT!

GUTENBERG (DOUG).

TOMORROW!

MONK (BUD).

TOMORROW!

MONK, HELVETICA & GUTENBERG (BUD & DOUG).

TOMORROW
IS TONIGHT!

> (*Spotlights fade on* **GUTENBERG** *and* **MONK,** *leaving only the* **HELVETICA** *hat lit.*)

HEVLETICA (BUD'S VOICE).

TOMORROW IS TO–

(*Spoken in rhythm.*) WHAT HAVE I DONE?

(**BUD** *and* **DOUG** *lean into* **HELVETICA**'*s spotlight.*)

BUD & DOUG. *(Spoken in rhythm.)*
INTERMISSION!

End of Act One

ACT TWO

*(**CHARLES** stands at his piano and, again, reads from a card.)*

CHARLES. Good evening again and welcome to everyone who snuck in during intermission. The Magnificent Seven is the tri-county's most awesome wedding band. We can also rock out your bar mitzvah, bat mitzvah, funeral, pet adoption or children's birthday party. And yes – we play "Baby Shark." Now, please welcome back to the stage – Doug Simon and Bud Davenport.*

[MUSIC NO. 10A – ACT TWO FANFARE]

*(The band plays as **BUD** and **DOUG** enter.)*

DOUG. Okay, here we go!

BUD. The second act!

DOUG. Is everyone back from the restrooms?

BUD. 'Cause I can go check.

DOUG. Broadway producers? Are you all back? Okay? So, Bud and I were talking during intermission and we thought you must be sitting there thinking to yourself, "I love this show more than any show I've ever seen ever...but who are these guys on stage?"

BUD. Yeah! Who *are* we?!

DOUG. We thought we'd take a second to tell you a little bit about *us*.

BUD. *(Joke.)* Or we!

---

* See alternate dialogue on page 90 for productions using only a pianist.

DOUG. Right! Us or we. Thank you – *Helvetica?!*

BUD. *(As* **HELVETICA**.*)* "You're welcome!"

> *(They laugh.)*

BUD. Just a little callback.

DOUG. We can be jokesters sometimes. But we also know how to be serious. Take it, Bud.

BUD. Now, my name is Mr. Bud Davenport. That you already know. But what you may not know – I'm forty-two, I'm single, and I love to make music.

DOUG. Watch out ladies!

BUD. Ha! Yes! I *am* looking for a wife. Other than Doug.

DOUG. Sometimes we act just like an old married couple!

> *(They laugh. And do a "bit.")*

BUD. I wish I was gay! But I'm just…not.

DOUG. It's okay, Bud. *(Beat.)* I am gay. My name is Doug Simon, I'm *approaching – (Big tight smile.)* – my early-to-mid-to-late-forties, I live in a studio apartment above an incredibly loud pet store, and I used to own a cat.

BUD. Until it died.

DOUG. Yes.

> *(Beat. They both look at the cat. Finally,* **DOUG** *recovers.)*

So… GUTENBERG! THE MUSICAL!

BUD. Why did we write it?!

DOUG. Great question. Now – it all started a few months after Fran McCallister and Bud's big "Don't Cry Frenchy" miracle.

BUD. It wasn't a miracle!

DOUG. *(Taken aback but pushing forward.)* Okay. Anyway, Bud was asked to stop being the organist at his church.

BUD. Yes. I got bit by the "Songwriting Bug." And I started improvising a lot during hymns.

DOUG. His "Amazing Grace" was...unrecognizable.

BUD. Thank you. My pastor said it was "not Christian" and "an abomination before the Lord."

DOUG. Needless to say, Bud needed some cheering up. So I said, "Hey Bud – let's sell your car and buy tickets to a Broadway show."

BUD. Now – I had never been to a Broadway show. But that weekend, we saw three. And a half.

DOUG. I got hungry.

BUD. Please don't tell us how *Hamilton* ends, we WILL go back.

DOUG. But after we went to Broadway, something shifted inside us.

BUD. Like a lunch that's so big it changes the shape of your body.

DOUG. Yes. Our lip sync concerts just weren't enough anymore.

BUD. We didn't want to pretend to sing someone else's songs. We wanted someone else to pretend to sing our songs.

DOUG. We were not successful right away.

BUD. No! Our first show was "Stephen King! The Musical!" It was every Stephen King book in one show.

DOUG. I still think that can work.

BUD. Totally.

DOUG. Our second show was a prequel to *Phantom of the Opera*.

BUD. How did he get that boat down there?!

DOUG. We never figured it out. So our next show was an original story about two gentlemen much like ourselves.

BUD. It was achingly autobiographical. I wrote thirty-five different songs about us.

DOUG. And I wrote lyrics for twelve of them. But we realized that original stories with original songs? Nobody wants that.

BUD. If your new musical isn't already a movie or a book or a fairy tale told from the lady's point-of-view, people will not sell their cars to see it.

DOUG. *(Excited, pitching it.)* Which brings us back to our Stephen King musical! It's *every* book! Even *Tommyknockers*!

BUD. *(Play-acting exasperation – calling back an old argument.)* Doug! Ya gotta let it go!

DOUG. *(Play-acting.)* But I don't want to!

(Then, flipping on a dime.) But I had to. Bud was right. So we started looking for a different book.

BUD. And then we thought – why not the very *first* book?

DOUG. And that was the Google search that led to the Google search that brought us all here tonight.

BUD & DOUG. "GUTENBERG! THE MUSICAL!"

BUD. The second act!

DOUG. Now – writing the second act of a musical is not easy.

BUD. Hats OFF to you, Elton John. But so many wonderful shows have been destroyed by a terrible second act.

DOUG. *West Side Story.*

BUD. *Jesus Christ Superstar.*

DOUG. *Oklahoma.*

BUD. *Godspell.*

DOUG. *Phantom of the Opera.*

BUD. The *Godspell* revival.

DOUG. All terrible!

BUD. Wonderful shows!

DOUG. We love those shows! But their second acts are all about ending stuff and wrapping up loose ends.

BUD. We like loose ends!

DOUG. Life is loose ends! That's why we didn't worry about trying to wrap up the story in a nice, shiny bow.

BUD. A story's not a present!

DOUG. It's nothing like a present. But if it was, we'd want to give it to you.

BUD. Maybe so you could take it to Broadway! Hey, speaking of stories, Doug – where did we leave off with the his-*story*-cal tale of Mr. Johann Gutenberg?

DOUG. Well, at the end of the first act, Monk and Helvetica *destroyed* the printing press.

BUD. But Gutenberg doesn't know that, and Helvetica feels horrible about it.

DOUG. She made a mistake.

BUD. Sometimes we all make mistakes.

DOUG. Act Two.

BUD. *(Stage direction.)* Second Prologue: *(He gestures to* **CHARLES***)*

[MUSIC NO. 11 – SECOND PROLOGUE]

DOUG. *(Stage direction.)* The Streets of Schlimmer. It is early in the morning. So early, the dirt streets are still covered with yesterday's vegetables. The stage is filled with doom. Also fog. Bootblack and Daughter meet on the street.

DAUGHTER (BUD).
BOOTBLACK

BOOTBLACK (DOUG).
DAUGHTER

DAUGHTER (BUD).
HAD A BAD DREAM LAST NIGHT

BOOTBLACK (DOUG). *(Spoken in rhythm.)*
TELL ME MORE.

DAUGHTER (BUD).
GUTENBERG
WAS SAD AND CRYING
IT WAS HORRIFYING

BOOTBLACK (DOUG).   **DAUGHTER (BUD).**
I HAD THAT DREAM TOO!   OOH!

BOOTBLACK (DOUG).
WE HAD THE SAME DREAM

DAUGHTER (BUD).
THE VERY SAME DREAM

BOOTBLACK (DOUG).
THEN GUTENBERG
BECAME AN EAGLE
AND ATTACKED A SEAGULL

DAUGHTER (BUD).
OH, THAT'S NOT LIKE MY DREAM

BOOTBLACK (DOUG).
(*Acting out the fight.*)
EAGLE, SEAGULL

DAUGHTER (BUD).
In my dream,   EAGLE, SEAGULL
Gutenberg's skin fell
off so he was just a   EAGLE, SEAGULL
skeleton. Then he
danced and it was scary   EAGLE, SEAGULL
but also erotic.

BOOTBLACK (DOUG).
DREAMS ARE WEIRD

DAUGHTER (BUD).
AND DISTURBING

BOOTBLACK (DOUG).
VERY DISCONCERTING

DAUGHTER (BUD).
HERE, I'LL DO THE DANCE

DAUGHTER (BUD).
(*Doing skeleton dance.*)
SEXY, SCARY

BOOTBLACK (DOUG).
An eagle is more   SEXY, SCARY
powerful than a seagull.
But in my dream, the   SEXY, SCARY
seagull had a knife. It
was terrifying! But also   SEXY, SCARY
erotic.

DAUGHTER (BUD).
THIS SEEMS BAD

BOOTBLACK (DOUG).
BUT WE CAN'T BE TOO SURE

BOOTBLACK & DAUGHTER (DOUG & BUD).
> DREAMS PREDICT THE FUTURE
> WHAT DID THESE DREAMS MEAN?

> *(After applause, **BUD** and **DOUG** address the audience:)*

BUD. That was a nightmare!

DOUG. People like me and Bud call a scene like that "foreshadowing."

BUD. *(For audience's benefit – infomercial.)* But Doug – what is foreshadowing?

DOUG. Well, I'll tell you...later! Hit it!

[MUSIC NO. 12 – WORDS, WORDS, WORDS]

(Stage direction.) Act Two, Scene One: An old-timey bar called The Rusty German! The roof is made of dirty thatch. The floor is covered in peanut shells.

BUD. *(Stage direction.)* Gutenberg sits at the bar. He is drunk.

GUTENBERG (DOUG).
> I AM DRUNK!
> I HAVE BEEN DRINKING WINE AND MEAD
> AND NOW MY FACE IS NUMB

> *(**DRUNK #1** enters. **GUTENBERG** calls to him.)*

> DRUNK! I CAN'T WAIT TILL YOU LEARN TO READ

DRUNK #1 (BUD). Do what?

GUTENBERG (DOUG).
> IT'S NOT YOUR FAULT THAT YOU'RE DUMB
> BUT THANKS TO *ME* YOU'LL SOON BE SMART

DRUNK #1 (BUD). Whoa! Gutenberg's drunk!

GUTENBERG (DOUG). I *am* drunk! For the last time.

DRUNK #1 (BUD). Oh no!

GUTENBERG (DOUG). That's right, Drunk! After tonight, ol' Gutenberg's not drinking wine anymore. I'm drinking words.

DRUNK #1 (BUD). You can't drink words!

GUTENBERG (DOUG). Not so fast there, Drunk!

WORDS CAN TAKE ON ANY FORM OR SHAPE

DRUNK #1 (BUD). You've gone insane.

GUTENBERG (DOUG).
(Shouted in rhythm.) NO!
WORDS ARE LIKE WINE FROM A BETTER GRAPE

DRUNK #1 (BUD). Huh?

GUTENBERG.
THE GRAPE OF YOUR BRAIN

DRUNK #1 (BUD). Oh!

GUTENBERG (DOUG).
WORDS ARE SO SWEET

DRUNK #1 (BUD).
WITH ICE OR JUST NEAT

GUTENBERG & DRUNK #1 (DOUG & BUD).
WE STOMP 'EM WITH BOTH FEET!

GUTENBERG (DOUG).
I'M GONNA GET DRUNK OFF OF WORDS
I'M GONNA COME HOME LATE!
I'M GONNA STINK OF WORDS!

GUTENBERG & DRUNK #1 (DOUG & BUD).
WINE IS AWF'LLY FINE
BUT REALLY WINE IS JUST A WORD
WORDS, WORDS, WORDS

DRUNK #1 (BUD). But if we're drinking words, then what are we gonna eat?

GUTENBERG (DOUG). *(Profound.)* I don't know. Maybe we can eat...dreams!

DRUNK #1 (BUD). Wow...

GUTENBERG (DOUG). I'm gonna get a drink.

DRUNK #1 (BUD). Great idea.

DRUNK #2 (DOUG). Hey, what's happenin'?

DRUNK #1 (BUD). Gutenberg's talking about eating dreams and getting drunk off of words.

DRUNK #2 (DOUG). That sounds stupid!

DRUNK #1 (BUD). It's not! Words make you feel all tingly inside!

DRUNK #2 (DOUG). *(Almost like a vaudeville routine.)* But that's what alcohol does!

DRUNK #1 (BUD). Yes, but words do it without the crippling chemical addiction.

DRUNK #2 (DOUG). *(This is the punch line.)* That's the part I don't like.

DRUNK #1 (BUD).
    WELL, THEN
    PULL UP A SEAT

DRUNK #2 (DOUG).
    THIS IS A TREAT!

TWO DRUNKS (BUD & DOUG).
    GUESS WE SHOULD REPEAT –
    WE'RE GONNA GET DRUNK OFF OF WORDS

DRUNK #1 (BUD).
    I'M GONNA START A FIGHT!

DRUNK #2 (DOUG).
    I'M GONNA VOMIT WORDS!

TWO DRUNKS (BUD & DOUG).
> WINE IS AWF'LLY FINE BUT REALLY WINE IS JUST A WORD
> WORDS, WORDS, WORDS

BUD. *(Stage direction.)* Helvetica enters.

HELVETICA (BUD).
> GUTENBERG!

GUTENBERG (DOUG).
> WHAT?

HELVETICA (BUD).
> I'VE GOT TO SAY –

GUTENBERG (DOUG).
> HEY!

HELVETICA (BUD).
> CAN I GET A SECOND CHANCE?

GUTENBERG (DOUG). I don't know what you're talking about.

HELVETICA (BUD).
> I'VE DONE SOMETHING REALLY AWFUL!

GUTENBERG (DOUG).
> COME ON HELVETICA –

> Let's dance!

BUD. *(Stage direction.)* DANCE BREAK!

> (**BUD** *and* **DOUG** *do a choreographed dance as
> the* **TWO DRUNKS.***)*

DOUG. *(Stage direction.)* They waltz!

> (**BUD** *and* **DOUG** *toss a hat to each other so
> that* **DOUG** *is wearing the* **GUTENBERG** *hat
> and holding* **HELVETICA**, *and* **BUD** *is wearing*
> **DRUNK #1** *and holding* **DRUNK #2.** *They each
> waltz with their hat partner.)*

BUD. *(Stage direction.)* Eventually the music slows and Gutenberg holds Helvetica close.

> (**BUD** *and* **DOUG** *spin towards each other –* **DOUG** *puts the* **HELVETICA** *hat on* **BUD**'s *head. They are in a spotlight. Perhaps there is a mirror ball making it feel almost dream-like.)*

GUTENBERG (DOUG). Hello.

HELVETICA (BUD). I don't understand.

GUTENBERG (DOUG). Wine can make you do crazy things.

HELVETICA (BUD). Before we danced...you said my name.

GUTENBERG (DOUG). Yes – that's because I love you.

HELVETICA (BUD). Stew! Female lamb stew!

GUTENBERG (DOUG). No! I mean, yes – but I also love you.

Y-O-U.

HELVETICA (BUD).
WHY OH ME?

GUTENBERG (DOUG). Heh Heh. You can't read.

> *(He kisses her on the forehead. Then a sudden mood change. He is angry.)*

You're fired!

HELVETICA (BUD). What?!

GUTENBERG (DOUG). I'm firing you as my grape stomper – but I want to hire you...as my wife.

HELVETICA (BUD). Oh Gutenberg, I – I – I... I can't! I've done something awful!

BUD. *(Stage direction.)* Helvetica leaves the bar in a tizzy!

HELVETICA (BUD). I'm in a tizzy!

> *(She leaves.)*

GUTENBERG (DOUG). Where are you going?! Where are you going?!

BUD. *(Stage direction.)* SECOND DANCE BREAK!

DOUG. *(Stage direction.)* The entire cast rushes on stage and Gutenberg is sucked into the madness.

> (**BUD** *and* **DOUG** *illustrate the following cast movements by puppeteering the hats.)*

BUD. *(Stage direction.)* Some do wild leaps in the air!

> (**BUD** *throws two hats.)*

DOUG. *(Stage direction.)* Some do flips!

> (**DOUG** *flips two hats in the air.)*

BUD. *(Stage direction.)* Some do somersaults.

> (**BUD** *makes two hats do a somersault.)*

DOUG. *(Stage direction.)* Some do handstands.

> (**DOUG** *holds two hats upside down like they are walking on their hands.)*

BUD. *(Stage direction.)* Some chicken fight in the corner.

> (**BUD** *makes two hats fight.)*

DOUG. *(Stage direction.)* And the grizzled, old Narrator soars above it all.

> (**DOUG** *tosses a hat across the stage.)*

The entire cast joins hands to form a chorus line.

> (**BUD** *and* **DOUG** *reveal a clothesline with hats tied to it. They each hold an end and extend it across the stage at head-height so the audience could easily imagine a chorus line.)*

> *(Note: Feel free to include as many of the non-principal characters as you want.* **GUTENBERG** *should be in the center. Also on one end of the line there should be a hat that says "BILLY.")*
>
> *(In time with the music,* **DOUG** *gives his end of the clothesline to* **BUD** *and steps into the line to wear the* **GUTENBERG** *hat tied to the line. They form a full chorus line with* **DOUG** *wearing the* **GUTENBERG** *hat in the center. He kicks in time to the music.)*

GUTENBERG & EVERYONE (DOUG & BUD).
> WE'RE GONNA GET DRUNK OFF OF WORDS
> SOMEONE ELSE SHOULD DRIVE
> BECAUSE WE'RE DRUNK OFF WORDS
> WINE IS AWF'LLY FINE
> BUT REALLY WINE IS JUST A WORD
> WORDS, WORDS, WORDS

> *(After applause,* **BUD** *and* **DOUG** *address the audience:)*

BUD. That was our big Act Two opener!

DOUG. We sure hope it lived up to any expectations you might have built up in the toilet. Now, did you notice how in that song Gutenberg kept singing about getting drunk off of words?

BUD. *(For the audience's benefit – infomercial.)* Hey, Doug! Does that mean what I think it means?

DOUG. I don't know, Bud. It's called a metaphor.

BUD. *(For the audience's benefit – infomercial.)* But what is a metaphor?

DOUG. Well, a metaphor is when you say one thing, and mean something else, but you're not lying. Now when we started writing the opening to Act Two, we knew

Gutenberg needed to have a lot of fun. And pretty much the funnest thing you can ever do is get drunk.

BUD. Doug used to get drunk a lot.

DOUG. Yep. My name is Doug Simon and I was an alcoholic. For one summer.

BUD. He slept in my yard.

DOUG. Yes. I learned that being an alcoholic…is expensive. Now – not only was that song about Gutenberg drinking delicious, delicious alcohol. We also saw Helvetica in that song and I'm pretty sure Gutenberg said he loved her. And then she ran away. I wonder where she went. *(Stage direction.)* Scene Two: The Church on the Hill.

[MUSIC NO. 12A – CHURCH ON THE HILL UNDERSCORE]

Monk has been taking confession from that awful flower girl. They are having way too much fun.

MONK (BUD). We are done here, Flower Girl. You are completely without sin.

LI'L NAZI GIRL (DOUG). Thank you!

MONK (BUD). No no no, thank *you* Flower Girl, for these beautiful flowers.

LI'L NAZI GIRL (DOUG). Alright, have a great weekend!

MONK (BUD). Okay. Bye.

> *(They laugh together somewhat maniacally.)*

BUD. *(Stage direction.)* Flower Girl exits. Helvetica enters.

HELVETICA (DOUG). Monk! I've got to speak with you! Gutenberg's press! We've got to fix it!

MONK (BUD). Poor, poor Helvetica! I'm afraid the Bible says there are no second chances.

HELVETICA (DOUG). It does?

MONK (BUD). Yes. Towards the end.

BUD. *(Stage direction.)* Young Monk enters.

YOUNG MONK (DOUG). Sir! Sir! Mr. Gutenberg! He's here! He wants to see you!

HELVETICA (DOUG). He's come to rescue me!

> (**MONK** *cackles –)*

MONK (BUD). Foolish wench! You've lured my nemesis directly into my clutches. Young Monk! Take Helvetica and lock her in the tower!

HELVETICA (DOUG). What?!

YOUNG MONK (DOUG). Why?

> (**MONK** *throws a pencil and stabs* **YOUNG MONK. YOUNG MONK** *screams in ridiculous pain.)*

MONK (BUD). Because I said so!

YOUNG MONK (DOUG). You are SUCH a bad monk!

MONK (BUD). You have no idea.

YOUNG MONK (DOUG). I have some idea.

BUD. *(Stage directions.)* Young Monk and Helvetica exit. Gutenberg enters.

GUTENBERG (DOUG). Hey. Nice church.

MONK (BUD). Well, well, well – you must be Gutenberg.

GUTENBERG (DOUG). Correctamundo! But call me Johann – Johann Gutenberg.

MONK (BUD). Well Mister Johann Gutenberg, what brings you to my church on the hill?

GUTENBERG (DOUG). This big Bible. Last night I invented the printing press.

MONK (BUD). *(Knowing, devious.)* Oh *really*?

GUTENBERG (DOUG). Yep! And now I want to print the Bible with it. I'm gonna call it "The Gutenberg Bible."

MONK (BUD). *(Aside.)* Ha! He must not know the printing press has been destroyed. Perhaps I can turn him to... the Monk Side.

[MUSIC CUE NO. 13 – MONK WITH ME]

(To **GUTENBERG**.*)* Tell me, Johann Gutenberg – you ever thought about working for the church?

GUTENBERG (DOUG). I did once. Seemed pretty boring.

MONK (BUD). No Johann Gutenberg! Monking is power!

MONK WITH ME
COME WORK HERE
I THINK YOU'LL LIKE IT
WE'VE GOT A CAT!

GUTENBERG (DOUG). *(He pets it.)* Aww!

MONK (BUD).
PLUS FREE LUNCH!
DELICIOUS!
LOAVES AND FISHES
HERE – TASTE THAT

*(***GUTENBERG*** takes a bite and loves it –)*

GUTENBERG (DOUG). Mmmm!

I USUALLY EAT LAMB AND STEW
MAYBE I LIKE FISH TOO?

*(***MONK*** laughs – his plan is working –)*

MONK (BUD). Ha ha ha ha!
MONK WITH ME
THE CLOTHES HERE?
IT'S ALL ROBES HERE!
(Spoken in rhythm.) DON'T THAT FEEL SOFT?

GUTENBERG (DOUG). *(Trying on the robe.)* Ooh!

MONK (BUD).
> IT'S REAL SILK
> FROM CHINA!
> THERE'S NOTHING FINER
> *(Spoken in rhythm.)* NOW TAKE IT OFF.

GUTENBERG (DOUG). But I want it!

MONK (BUD).
> THEN
> MONK WITH ME
> MY FRIEND
> YEAH! WE'RE MONKIN' FOR GOD NOW!
> MONK WITH ME
> MY FRIEND!

GUTENBERG (DOUG).
> I'M TEMPTED BY THIS MONK LIFESTYLE
> BUT I WANT SOMETHING MORE WORTHWHILE
> A WORLD WHERE EV'RYONE CAN READ
> CAN I STILL DO THAT, MONK?

MONK (BUD).
> IT'S BETTER IF THE WORLD CAN'T READ
> GOD IS WHAT THE PEOPLE NEED
> THAT GOD, HE COULD BE US... OR WE!
> OH GUTENBERG! MONK WITH –

GUTENBERG (DOUG). No! Oh Monk, don't you see? We're different. You believe in God. I believe in...stuff. God and stuff don't mix. They're like bugs and beautiful skin. Plus, let's face it – you are a terrible monk.

MONK (BUD). Choose your words very carefully, Johann Gutenberg.

GUTENBERG (DOUG). Words? Yes! I almost forgot.

MONK (BUD). What –?

GUTENBERG (DOUG). WORDS! Yes! Like the words in this Bible!

MONK (BUD). No!

GUTENBERG (DOUG). Words are why I came here!

I BELIEVE IN MY WORDS
I BELIEVE IN MY PRESS
I BELIEVE IN A READING GERMANY!
NOW YOU WANT ME TO MONK
AND THROW THAT AWAY

GUTENBERG (DOUG).

I THINK IT'S TIME TO GO   **MONK (BUD).**

DO NOT TELL ME...
MY ANSWER, MONK, IS NO!   DO NOT TELL ME NO!
(Spoken in rhythm.) NO!

(Spoken in rhythm.) NO!

*(**MONK** suddenly seems incredibly powerful, controlling objects with a wave of his hand.)*

MONK (BUD). Doors lock! Windows close! You're not going anywhere, Johann Gutenberg.

GUTENBERG (DOUG). Yes I am! And I'm taking this huge Bible with me. *(Grabs the Bible.)* Ah! It feels like... goodness!

*(**MONK** roars! **GUTENBERG** holds the Bible above his head.)*

The only thing better than this feeling would be mass-producing this feeling.

MONK (BUD). You better get your mind off of words, Johann Gutenberg. Why, don't you want to go to heaven?

GUTENBERG (DOUG). Heaven?

MONK (BUD). Yes! Heaven. Where do *you* think people go when they die?

GUTENBERG (DOUG). I don't know. I guess I think most people turn into dirt. But some people...turn into statues.

MONK (BUD). *Statues?*

GUTENBERG (DOUG). Yes! I want my statue to be me riding on a dragon...nursing a baby.

MONK (BUD). Oh! Johann Gutenberg – there are no statues in heaven!

GUTENBERG (DOUG). THEN I DON'T WANT TO GO THERE!!!

>   *(A tense beat. **MONK** is shocked and a little thrown.)*

MONK (BUD). What?! But...everybody wants to go to heaven. That's what gives me my power.

GUTENBERG (DOUG).
OH MONK, YOU CANNOT UNDERSTAND
THE WORLD HAS CHANGED FOR HUMAN MAN
THINKING, READING, THAT'S THE PLAN!
YOUR MONK WAYS ARE OLD NEWS
AND I WILL NEVER MONK WITH –

Hey Monk, I'm taking this Bible.

>   *(He takes the Bible, starts out, turns back –)*

But Monk, I hope we can be...friends.

>   *(He leaves. **MONK** reels.)*

MONK (BUD). Friends?! Ridiculous! Impossible! The Bible says a Monk shall not have...friends.

>   *(Suddenly softening.)*

Then again, I wouldn't mind having a buddy I could talk to every now and then. We crack open a little communion wine? Watch a joust? Maybe bait a bear? Oooh, I love to bait a bear. But aw heck, for that to happen, the whole world would have to change.

(Getting an idea.)

Then again...what if it did...change?

A WORLD WITH NO MORE MONKING
NO HEAVEN AND NO HELL
AND I DON'T WORK FOR SATAN
HOW I HATE THAT SULFUR SMELL
IF CHANGE IS A'COMIN' LIKE JOHANN SAYS
LORD, COULD I CHANGE AS WELL?
I'D HAVE NO POWER BUT I WOULD BE GOOD!

(He lifts his arms to heaven as if in prayer. Then – the music shifts. **MONK** *is suddenly angry.)*

No!

(He flips off God.)

What am I saying? God is my enemy. And being good is the exact opposite of what I want.

THERE IS NO GOOD IN ME!
THERE'S HAUNTED GERMAN WOOD IN ME!
AND GUTENBERG IS GONNA SEE
THE WORLD
WILL
MONK
WITH
ME!

(After applause –)

BUD. Now Doug, are my ears playing tricks on me or did Monk sing a little bit of "Haunted German Wood" again?

DOUG. Your ears are perfect, Bud. It's called a motif.

BUD. *(For the audience's benefit – infomercial.)* But Doug, what is a motif?

DOUG. A motif is when you use the same music over and over again – but it's not lazy.

BUD. Now we know what you're probably wondering, and the answer is yes. That scene was inspired by *Star Wars*.

DOUG. But that scene was also inspired…by reality.

BUD. There sure are an awful lot of people talking about God these days.

DOUG. Yep. But there's also a lot of people talking about stuff.

BUD. It's a constant debate.

DOUG. Constant.

BUD. And there's some people that believe you don't even need *stuff*. They think all you need is the Bible.

DOUG. We think that's dumb. Is the sound of a child's laughter in the Bible? Is the beauty of a sunset in the Bible? What about bacon?

BUD. Now don't get us wrong, we love the Bible.

DOUG. Both parts.

BUD. There are so many animals in there!

DOUG. And Gutenberg loved the Bible too. That's why he wanted everyone to read it.

BUD. Which is exactly why Monk doesn't want him to have it.

DOUG. No, see Monk wants *power*. When you know something other people don't – that's power.

BUD. That's why Doug and I tell each other everything.

DOUG. Yep! We know all of each other's deepest, darkest secrets and you don't.

BUD. And that's power!

DOUG. But we don't want to have power over you, so we thought it would be fun if we told you one secret thing about ourselves. Take it, Bud.

BUD. I'm a virgin.

DOUG. What!?

BUD. I've done everything else, but I'm saving that for marriage.

(**DOUG** *crosses to him, concerned –*)

DOUG. You never told me that. You're a very old virgin, Bud –

BUD. I know, but wait – I thought I was supposed to tell the audience a secret that even you don't know?

DOUG. Oh. Right. I see. Okay. Yeah, we can do that. I'm just gonna have to...dig a little deeper.

BUD. Do it, Doug. Dig deeper.

DOUG. Alright... Let's see... Something I've never told you?

BUD. Something brand new, Doug. Hit me.

(*A beat.* **DOUG** *sighs –*)

DOUG. I killed my mother.

BUD. What!?

DOUG. Okay, so, ever since I was a little boy, my mom wanted me to be a doctor. So one day, I got up my courage and I told her, "I don't want to be a doctor, mom! I want to follow my dreams." And she said, "That's not a job, Doug! You gotta put food on the table! You can't eat dreams!" Then we got in a huge fight –

BUD. And that's when you killed her?

DOUG. No. Years later, she got sick and…she needed a doctor. But I wasn't a doctor, 'cause I was off…eating dreams. And musical theatre can do a lotta things, but it can't cure lupus.

BUD. Wait, Doug, did she not have health insurance?

DOUG. *("How ridiculous!")* Ha! We're not made of money!

BUD. Oh Doug. That's not your fault, that's America's fault. America killed your mom.

DOUG. Thanks, Bud.

BUD. *(To the audience.)* So those are our secrets. I'm a virgin and Doug thinks he killed his mom.

DOUG. And now you all know that.

BUD. So you all have the power.

DOUG. And that's exactly what Gutenberg wanted. But you know doesn't have power?

BUD. Helvetica.

DOUG. That's why she's about to sing our big eleven o'clock number.

BUD. *(For the audience's benefit – infomercial.)* But what is an eleven o'clock number, Doug?

DOUG. Well, in olden times, Broadway shows were very long and very boring, so by the time the leading lady had her big emotional climax? The audience was home in bed.

BUD. That's why we're singing our eleven o'clock number at –

    (Checks his watch.)

  – [READS EXACT TIME].

DOUG. *(Stage direction.)* Scene Three:

[MUSIC NO. 14 – GO TO HELL]

Monk's Evil Tower! It is dark and dank.

BUD. The floor is covered with Rats. And Feces.

> (**BUD** *holds up two hats that say* **RATS** *and* **FECES** *and throws them on the ground.*)

Helvetica sits at the window, overlooking the moon.

HELVETICA (DOUG).
I'M IN A TOWER WITH RATS AND SOME FECES
THE MAN I ADORE IS SO CLOSE AND YET SO FAR
IF HE WERE HERE, I WOULD SAY "DON'T RELEASE ME
'CAUSE MY HEART IS ONE BIG SCAR
I'M THE STUPID, GERMAN WENCH WHO BETRAYED YA,
    BABY"
I'M RIGHT WHERE I OUGHTA BE
TELL 'EM THE RATS IN HERE ATE ME

HISTORY'S PAVED WITH THE HEARTS OF THE STUPID
HEAVEN IS SAVED FOR THE SOULS WHO HAVE NO SIN
I THOUGHT I WAS BRAVE WHEN I SAID "HEY" TO CUPID
BUT I WON'T DO THAT AGAIN
'CAUSE NOW I'LL NEVER HAVE A FRIEND OR LOVER
SO MAYBE I OUGHTA GO
MAYBE I
MIGHT AS WELL GO TO HELL

MIGHT AS WELL
MIGHT AS WELL GO TO HELL
MIGHT AS WELL
MIGHT AS WELL GO TO HELL

> (**HELVETICA** *picks up the cat.*)

MY MOMMA TOLD ME THAT HELL WAS A BAD PLACE
WITH NO PRETTY KITTIES
TO CUDDLE WHEN YOU'RE LOW

HELVETICA (DOUG).

> WHEN I AM DEAD I WILL SURE MISS YOUR CAT FACE
> BUT I GOOFED UP, AND I KNOW
> I WILL NEVER LEAVE MEDIEVAL DEATH ROW
> SO MAYBE I OUGHTA GO
> MAYBE I MIGHT AS WELL GO TO HELL

> > (**HELVETICA** *drops the cat.*)

HELVETICA (DOUG).	**RATS (BUD).**
MIGHT AS WELL	TCH TCH TCH TCH TCH
	TCH TCH TCH TCH TCH
MIGHT AS WELL GO	TCH TCH TCH TCH TCH
TO HELL	
RATS! SING WITH ME!	TCH TCH TCH TCH TCH

> > (**BUD** *holds two hats with the word* **RAT** *on them.*
> > *He puppeteers them for the rest of the song.*)

RATS (BUD).

> MIGHT AS WELL
> MIGHT AS WELL GO
> MIGHT AS WELL GO TO HELL

HELVETICA (DOUG).	**RATS (BUD).**
MIGHT AS WELL	MIGHT AS WELL
	MIGHT AS WELL GO
MIGHT AS WELL GO	MIGHT AS WELL GO
TO HELL	TO HELL
I WANT TO DIE	OOOOH!
BUT SHOULD I TRY	
TO KILL MYSELF?	
I DON'T KNOW!	WAAH!
TO BE OR NOT TO BE...	WAH WAH WAH WAH WAH
ME?	WAH WAH
I'VE GOTTA DO IT!	

BUD. *(Stage direction.)* Helvetica bends the bars, steps out
  on the ledge and prepares to jump.

(**DOUG** *mimes all of this as* **BUD** *describes it. Then he jumps. The flying should be accomplished through whatever creative means you want to employ – though it should be pretty lame.*)

HELVETICA (DOUG). I'm flying!

BUD. *(Stage direction.)* Helvetica soars over the town of Schlimmer.

HELVETICA (DOUG). Goodbye rats! Goodbye feces! Hello Schlimmer!! Whee!! It's beautiful!

(*She spins around – the bars return.*)

But it's not real.

I'm still in my tower.

I HAVE BETRAYED YOU, MY BEAUTIFUL HAMLET
AND WHEN I SAY HAMLET, I'M TALKIN' 'BOUT MY TOWN
'CAUSE THERE ARE TWO MEANINGS OF THE WORD
    HAMLET
SO MAYBE I OUGHTA DROWN
OR PUT MY BODY IN THE GROUND
'CAUSE I LET EV'RYBODY DOWN
I'M JUST A CRYING CLOWN
WEARING A PAINTED FROWN
I HEAR A SCARY SOUND
IT'S A THREE-HEADED HOUND!
FOUND WITH A BROWN, ROUND CROWN IN HELL!

(*The* **RATS** *climb all over* **HELVETICA**. *She loves them.*)

RATS (BUD).
MIGHT AS WELL
MIGHT AS WELL GO
MIGHT AS WELL GO TO HELL

HELVETICA (DOUG).	**RATS (BUD).**
MIGHT AS WELL	MIGHT AS WELL
COME AND GET ME	MIGHT AS WELL GO
SATAN!	MIGHT AS WELL GO
	TO HELL
I WANNA BE WITH YOU!	
	MIGHT AS WELL
I WANT YOUR HORNS	MIGHT AS WELL GO
INSIDE ME!	MIGHT AS WELL GO
	TO HELL
I WANNA LIVE WITH YOU!	
	MIGHT AS WELL
IN HELL!	MIGHT AS WELL GO
	MIGHT AS WELL GO
	MIGHT AS WELL
GO TO HELL	

(After applause –)

BUD. *(Very honest and overwhelmed – this is not "on-script.")* Doug, I would like to say something. This has been the most important night of my life.

DOUG. *(Sharing the moment with* **BUD.***)* This is the most important night of *my* life!

BUD. I'm never gonna forget this night. In fact – I am going to tell my grandkids about it.

DOUG. I'm gonna tell my grand*parents*!

BUD. Until tonight, I had no idea what it felt like to open up your chest and show an audience your heart.

DOUG. It hurts. But it's the good kind of hurt.

BUD. Doug...what if this is it?

DOUG. What?

BUD. We rented a theatre, we spent all of Uncle Travis's money...what if no one wants our show and this was all for nothing?

(A long beat as they both struggle with this horrible notion. Then, **DOUG** *rallies –)*

DOUG. Well...maybe it is all for nothing, but dammit...we got this far, didn't we?

(Gestures to the audience.)

Look out there! Look at all those people. Hell, look at us! *None of this makes any sense!* But here we are. And if this show doesn't happen, well, then...we'll write another one. And another one! 'Cause my mom can't be right! Dammit, we are gonna die doing what we love.

BUD. *(Comforted.)* Just like Uncle Travis...

(Then.)

Hey Doug – do you know why I get all squishy when you say my "Don't Cry Frenchy" song was a miracle?

DOUG. Honestly? I really don't. I think it's weird.

BUD. It's 'cause the miracle came later. All I did was make up a song. You're the one who said I should write it down. You're the one who said we should write musicals. And...you're the one who wouldn't let us quit. You never let us quit. Even that night I ate too much Papa Johns and threw up all over my piano, you never, ever let us quit. That's the reason we're here. That's the miracle.

DOUG. *(Touched.)* Bud, that's not... All I did was...

BUD. Now look who's getting squishy.

*(***DOUG*** smiles, exhales. A moment of shared admiration, then –)*

DOUG. Hey...maybe there's two miracles.

*(***BUD*** nods. He likes that idea.)*

DOUG. And you know what? I don't think this is the end. Next time this show happens, we're gonna be sitting out there where *they* are. *(He indicates the audience.)* Wearing tuxedos. On opening night. On Broadway!

BUD. *(Getting on board.)* Yeah...yeah! And there'll be a giant set with real dirt streets and real animals and... and...instead of two drunks – there'll be like a hundred drunks!

DOUG. Like a thousand drunks!

BUD. Like a million! *(Beat.)* Like a million drunks. I'm so proud of you, Doug.

DOUG. I'm proud of you too, Bud.

> *(They hug. A moment of awkward exuberance. They turn to address the audience, but* **DOUG** *seems lost.)*

What – um – what was I supposed to talk about here?

BUD. Suicide

DOUG. Suicide! Yes.

> *(Back on script.)* Now – did you notice how in that song, Helvetica kept singing about wanting to kill herself?

BUD. Suicide is an act of desperation.

DOUG. That's why it's perfect for a musical! Think about it!

BUD. *Les Miz*?

DOUG. Javert.

BUD. *Miss Saigon*?

DOUG. Kim.

BUD. *The Music Man*

DOUG. Shipoopi. But Helvetica doesn't kill herself. She stays in Monk's evil tower.

> (**DOUG** *readies hats for the next song as* **BUD** *continues –*)

BUD. Now, there is a scene that's not in the show – because it is just too intense. And that's the scene where the Monk tortures Helvetica. I'm sure you can imagine it though.

> (*He acts it out as he talks.*)

> (*Note: The following speech is* **DOUG** *and* **BUD**'s *way of buying time for* **DOUG** *to prepare the hats for the next song. But* **BUD** *clearly relishes telling this story.*)

Helvetica curled up in the corner of that dark room. Water dripping. The roof is made of dirty thatch. Monk enters, a sinister smile on his face. Wearing his finest robes. He crosses to her. Swish. Swish. He reaches toward her. Is there a tender touch?

DOUG. (*Finished prepping.*) Ahem.

BUD. Are we ready? Okay, here we go. (*Stage directions.*) Scene Four: The next morning.

[MUSIC NO. 15 – FESTIVAL]

DOUG. (*Stage directions.*) Today is the day of the German celebration known as "Festival"!

BUD. (*Stage directions.*) Dawn is beginning to break over the town of Schlimmer. Beef Fat Trimmer strides forward through the stinky morning mist.

> (**BUD** *and* **DOUG** *are both wearing all the hats they will need for this song and the rest of the show. It should be a ridiculous sight – a tower of hats on both their heads.*)

BEEF FAT TRIMMER (DOUG).

> THE SUN IT RISES IN THE EAST
> I SMELL BREAD RISING WITH THE YEAST
> FOR TODAY IS NO ORDINARY DAY
> IT'S THE DAY OF FESTIVAL

DAUGHTER (BUD).	**BEEF FAT TRIMMER (DOUG).**
TODAY I DANCE	
	THE SUN IT RISES IN
AT THE FESTIVAL	THE EAST
IN LEDERHOSEN PANTS	
YEAH! THAT'S THE	I SMELL BREAD RISING
BEST OF ALL	WITH THE YEAST

DAUGHTER (BUD) & BEEF FAT TRIMMER (DOUG).

> FOR TODAY IS NO ORDINARY DAY
> IT'S THE DAY OF FESTIVAL

BUD. *(Stage direction.)* We see Gutenberg pulling a wagon with the printing press inside. It is covered with a sheet. He is going to the town square. He still does not know the press has been destroyed.

GUTENBERG (DOUG).

> THEY'LL GO NUTS!
> AND LIFT ME IN THEIR ARMS!
> WHEN I SHOW 'EM MY PRESS
> I'M TAKING TO FESTIVAL

> *(We see **HELVETICA** locked in Monk's Evil Tower.)*

HELVETICA (BUD).

> OH GUTENBERG I'M SORRY

GUTENBERG (DOUG).

> I'M SO PSYCHED

HELVETICA (BUD).

> FORGIVE ME!

GUTENBERG (DOUG).

I'LL BE EVEN MORE WELL-LIKED!

HELVETICA (BUD).

THE TOWN WILL HAVE HIS HEAD

ONCE THEY SEE THE PRINTING PRESS IS DEAD!

(**BUD** *and* **DOUG** *create the illusion of a quartet.*)

DAUGHTER (BUD).	HELVETICA (BUD).	BEEF FAT TRIMMER (DOUG).	GUTENBERG (DOUG).
TODAY I DANCE			
	OH, GUTENBERG.	THE SUN IT RISES IN THE –	
AT THE FEST–			GUTENBERG!
	WILL YOU EVER		GUTENBERG!
	FORGIVE ME		GUTENBERG!
LEDERHOSEN			GUTENBERG!
PANTS			GUTENBERG!
	I STOPPED YOUR PRESS	I SMELL BREAD RISING	
THAT'S THE		WITH THE –	
BEST			GUTENBERG!
	NOW I'M A		GUTENBERG!
	MESS		GUTENBERG!
			GUTENBERG!
			GUTENBERG!

DAUGHTER, HELVETICA, BEEF FAT TRIMMER & GUTENBERG (BUD & DOUG).

FOR TODAY IS NO ORDINARY DAY

IT'S THE DAY

DAUGHTER (BUD).

THE BLESSED DAY

DAUGHTER, HELVETICA, BEEF FAT TRIMMER & GUTENBERG (BUD & DOUG).

OF FESTIVAL

TWO DRUNKS (BUD & DOUG).

IT'S THE FESTIVAL!!!!!!

> *(Suddenly the whole town is alive with celebration. It's Festival! The* **TWO DRUNKS** *do a choreographed dance.)*

FESTIVAL
IT'S THE BEST OF ALL
IT'S THE CREST OF ALL
OUR DESIRES!

FESTIVAL
TAKE THE REST OF ALL
OF THE FESTIVALS
TO THE FIRES!

DRUNK #2 (DOUG).

THERE IS SO MUCH FOOD AND DRINK

DRUNK #1 (BUD).

IT'S JUST ENOUGH TO MAKE YOU THINK

DRUNK #2 (DOUG).

THAT WE SHOULD ALL BE TICKLED PINK

TWO DRUNKS (BUD & DOUG).

BUT UNTIL WE ARE, LET'S DANCE!

MONK (BUD).

DON'T FORGET I MET THE DEVIL
IN A HAUNTED GERMAN WOOD

I'M A TERRIBLE MONK, AND I GOT A PLAN!
AND IT'S HAPPENIN' LIKE IT SHOULD

NOW THE GIRL'S IN TROUBLE
AND THE PRESS IS RUBBLE
AND HIS GUTEN-BUBBLE'S GONNA BURST!

HA!

I'LL JUST WAIT AND SEE
WINE-MAN, MISTER G

AS THEY ROAST HIM
LIKE A BRATWURST

> (**MONK** *throws a pencil and stabs* **YOUNG MONK** *as he enters.* **YOUNG MONK** *screams in ridiculous pain.*)

YOUNG MONK (DOUG).
WHY DOES HE HAVE TO BE

MONK (BUD).
HA HA HA HA

YOUNG MONK (DOUG).
SO BAD?

> (*The* **LI'L NAZI GIRL** *enters giving out flowers from a basket.*)

LI'L NAZI GIRL (BUD).
WELL I'VE GOT DAFFODILS
AND SOME ROSES TOO
BUT YOU CAN'T HAVE ONE
BECAUSE YOU'RE A JEW!

> (**BUD** *points at someone in the audience and freezes on them. He stays frozen, staring right at them through the beginning of the following speech.*)

GUTENBERG (DOUG). *(Spoken in rhythm.)*
SHUT UP!

Oh Flower Girl! Why must you have this ridiculous hatred of the Jews? It's irrational and it's wrong.

> (**BUD** *breaks his freeze and moves upstage.*)

It hurts me to see my fellow townspeople acting this way.

[MUSIC NO. 15A – IT'S IRRATIONAL]

GUTENBERG (DOUG). Just think of where all this hatred could lead. Before you know it...we could be in the middle of a second world war. So I have something... under this sheet...that could unite us all.

> (**GUTENBERG** *pulls the sheet off the press to reveal it's just rubble. He is stunned.*)

BUD. *(Stage direction.)* Everyone gasps.

> (**BUD** *puppeteers his hats to make everyone gasp. Then –*)

> (**MONK** *appears.*)

MONK (BUD). Well, well, well – what have we here?

GUTENBERG (DOUG). It *was* a printing press.

MONK (BUD). A printing press? What's that for?

GUTENBERG (DOUG). It *was* going to change the world.

MONK (BUD). Get him!

> (*A solitary spotlight hits* **DOUG** *as a sinister chord rings out on the piano.*)

DOUG. *(Stage direction.)* The Townspeople converge and attack Gutenberg. They are filled with irrational mob mentality and soon collect wood, light a fire, and burn Gutenberg alive. Lights shift.

[MUSIC NO. 16 – WE EAT DREAMS]

> (*The lights shift.* **BUD** *and* **DOUG** *take a second to rearrange their hats and stack them on their heads for the epilogue.*)

BUD. *(Stage direction.)* The cast join hands and walk to the edge of the stage.

> (**BUD** *and* **DOUG** *go to opposite sides of the stage and pretend to hold hands with the other*

*characters as if they are all in a line. After they
speak, they take a step towards the center and
reveal the hat of the next character "in line.")*

BEEF FAT TRIMMER (DOUG). Gutenberg's death did not stop his dream.

DAUGHTER (BUD). His printing press was rebuilt, and used to print many things.

DRUNK #2 (DOUG). Like the Gutenberg Bible.

HELVETICA (BUD). And even the very playbills you hold in your hands.

YOUNG MONK (DOUG). But Gutenberg's dream of universal literacy remains unrealized.

DRUNK #1 (BUD). Many people still do not know how to read.

OLD NARRATOR (DOUG). And we're not just talkin' about children and blind people.

LI'L NAZI GIRL (BUD). Statistics tell us that more than half the people in this room cannot read.

DEAD BABY (DOUG). The struggle continues.

MONK (BUD). That's why the story of Gutenberg is an inspiration for us all!

GUTENBERG (DOUG). Because it's not the success that matters. It's the dream!

> *(**BUD** and **DOUG** finally reach each other.
> They take off their **MONK** and **GUTENBERG**
> hats to reveal hats that say **BUD** and **DOUG**
> respectively. Then they hold hands.)*

DOUG SIMON. Hi, we're the authors of this musical. I wrote the book.

BUD DAVENPORT. I wrote the music.

DOUG SIMON & BUD DAVENPORT. And we both wrote the lyrics.

DOUG SIMON. We wrote ourselves into the finale of this show because, like Gutenberg, we have dreams, too.

BUD DAVENPORT. And while the printing press may not have solved all the world's problems –

DOUG SIMON. *("Amiright?")* Nazis!

BUD DAVENPORT. We hope the story of the printing press did im*press* upon all of you the power of *our* dreams.

> *(They drop hands and move out of the "line" to sing the song.)*

DOUG SIMON.
LIFE CAN BE CRUEL
AND KINDA COLD

BUD DAVENPORT.
AND OFTEN NO ONE'S THERE
TO HOLD YOU WHEN YOU CRY

DOUG SIMON.
SO THOSE WHO HOPE MUST CLOSE THEIR EYES

BUD DAVENPORT.
AND TRUST A BRIGHTER FUTURE LIES

DOUG SIMON & BUD DAVENPORT.
IN DREAMS
WHERE OUR LITTLE LIVES ARE ROUNDED WITH A SLEEP
AND WHILE THE EMPTINESS WITHIN US MAY BE DEEP
WE SEE A DAY
WHEN HOPELESS MILLIONS ALL CAN SAY
WE EAT DREAMS

BUD DAVENPORT.	**DOUG SIMON.**
WE EAT DREAMS	WE EAT DREAMS
That's right.	I EAT THEM TOO
WE EAT DREAMS	WE EAT DREAMS
OH, DOH DEE YOH DOH DOH	I EAT THEM TOO
WE EAT DREAMS	

DOUG SIMON. We all want to eat dreams, don't we? Well we're here to tell you, my mom was wrong. You *can* eat dreams. And they're delicious! So don't just sit there, we want you to sing along with us, we're going to sing "we eat dreams," we want you to sing "we eat them too." Okay, here we go.

DOUG SIMON & BUD DAVENPORT.
WE EAT DREAMS

BUD DAVENPORT & AUDIENCE.
WE EAT THEM TOO

DOUG SIMON. Come on everybody!

DOUG SIMON & BUD DAVENPORT.
WE EAT DREAMS

BUD DAVENPORT & AUDIENCE.
WE EAT THEM TOO

DOUG SIMON. Okay, this time just the LOW voices.

DOUG SIMON & BUD DAVENPORT.
WE EAT DREAMS

BUD DAVENPORT & AUDIENCE.
WE EAT THEM TOO

DOUG SIMON. Bass! Baritone! Make it rumble!

DOUG SIMON & BUD DAVENPORT.
WE EAT DREAMS

BUD DAVENPORT & AUDIENCE.
WE EAT THEM TOO

DOUG SIMON. Now just HIGH voices!

DOUG SIMON & BUD DAVENPORT.
WE EAT DREAMS

BUD DAVENPORT & AUDIENCE.
WE EAT THEM TOO

DOUG SIMON. Sopranos! Altos! Tenors who want to show off!

DOUG SIMON & BUD DAVENPORT.
WE EAT DREAMS

BUD DAVENPORT & AUDIENCE.
WE EAT THEM TOO

DOUG SIMON. Okay, now just Broadway Producers!

DOUG SIMON & BUD DAVENPORT.
WE EAT DREAMS

> *(A* **BROADWAY PRODUCER** *stands up in the audience wearing a hat that says* **PRODUCER.** **BUD** *and* **DOUG** *are stunned and delighted. They did not stage this. It's a miracle.)*

BROADWAY PRODUCER.
I EAT THEM TOO

DOUG SIMON & BUD DAVENPORT.
WE EAT DREAMS

BROADWAY PRODUCER.
I EAT THEM TOO

> *(* **PRODUCER** *comes on stage and addresses* **BUD** *and* **DOUG.***)*

BROADWAY PRODUCER. Bud, Doug, this show is fantastic. I don't need to hear another note. I'm a famous Broadway Producer, and I hold in my hands a Broadway contract.

> *(He shows them and the audience a thick sheaf of papers clearly labeled: BROADWAY CONTRACT.)*

Congratulations, Bud & Doug! You've got your show!

> *(They embrace, then turn out together and sing!)*

DOUG SIMON, BUD DAVENPORT & BROADWAY PRODUCER.
WHERE OUR LITTLE LIVES ARE ROUNDED WITH A SLEEP
AND WHILE THE EMPTINESS WITHIN US MAY BE DEEP
WE SEE A DAY
WHEN HOPELESS MILLIONS ALL CAN SAY
WE EAT DREAMS

(**BROADWAY PRODUCER** *steps back and enjoys the final moment.*)

DOUG SIMON & BUD DAVENPORT.
WE EAT DREAMS

(*Lights fade out.*)

The End

[MUSIC NO. 17 – CURTAIN CALL]

[MUSIC NO. 18 – EXIT MUSIC]

ALTERNATE LINES IF YOU ARE PERFORMING THE SHOW WITH ONLY A PIANIST

Act One

(Pages 2–3)

DOUG. So as you can see, we need this to go well.

BUD. It has to.

DOUG. Now, before we get started, we do want to be professional, so over there at the piano, that is Charles.

CHARLES. Hello.

BUD & DOUG. Hi Charles!

DOUG. Charles is the pianist.

BUD. Yes. But he is a "professional musician." Hit it, Charles!

> (**CHARLES** *JAMS HARD – on a classic rock song. It's awesome.* **BUD** *dances. Then* **DOUG** *cuts them off with a conductor's flourish –)*

DOUG. STOP! STOP! STOP!

(Then, to audience.) If he plays even one more note we have to pay for the song.

BUD. And we have literally no more money.

Act Two

(Page 49)

CHARLES. Good evening again and welcome to everyone who snuck in during intermission. Now, please welcome back to the stage – Doug Simon and Bud Davenport.

PRODUCTION NOTES

This is ostensibly a reading of a musical. It should absolutely not be performed on anything resembling an appropriate set for the show-within-the-show. Every set piece and prop should be simple, functional, and expository. In other words, we should be able to easily believe they were created and/or chosen by Bud & Doug for this reading.

There are many challenges created by Bud and Doug performing their full-cast show by themselves. In addition to the solutions listed here and in the script, feel free to create your own clever and odd solutions for these moments.

THE HATS should be plain trucker hats, unembellished except for the name of the character hand-written on the front. Whenever Bud and Doug are playing a character in the show-within-the-show they should be wearing that character's hat. When speaking lines as themselves, or giving stage directions, they should not wear a hat. Much of the staging in the show will grow from this necessity. When appropriate, the authors suggest stacking the hats on top of each other before key sequences in the show, wearing many hats at once, and taking them off one at a time to reveal the characters as needed. The authors suggest the following labels for the hats:

GUTENBERG	**DRUNK #2**	**RAT**
MONK	**WOMAN**	**RAT**
HELVETICA	**DAUGHTER**	**RATS**
YOUNG MONK	**ANOTHER WOMAN**	**FECES**
BEEF FAT TRIMMER	**FRIEND**	**BUD**
BOOTBLACK	**DOCTOR**	**DOUG**
LI'L NAZI GIRL	**OLD NARRATOR**	**PRODUCER**
DRUNK #1	**DEAD BABY**	

TWO LARGE BOXES should be used to represent the BUCKET and the WINE PRESS/PRINTING PRESS/RUBBLE. As simply as possible the WINE PRESS box must become the PRINTING PRESS box and RUBBLE box (the Broadway production solved this problem by using multiple signs and magnets).

Feel free to use as many other props in the show as you see fit. Miming props and set pieces is also fine. Keep it simple, be resourceful, and have fun.